THE GUARDIANS *of* GA'HOOLE

... and then the forest of the Kingdom of Tyto seemed to grow
smaller and smaller and dimmer and dimmer in the night ...

GUARDIANS
of GA'HOOLE

BOOK ONE

The Capture

BY KATHRYN LASKY

SCHOLASTIC INC.

New York Toronto London Auckland
Sydney Mexico City New Delhi Hong Kong

ISBN 978-0-439-40557-7

Artwork by Richard Cowdrey
Design by Steve Scott
The text type was set in Golden Cockerel.

30   12 13 14 15 / 0

Printed in the U.S.A.   40

First printing, September 2003

To Ann Reit, Wise Owl, Great Flight Instructor
— K. L.

Contents

Prologue

The world spiraled, the needles of the old fir tree blurred against the night sky and then there was a sickening sensation as the forest floor raced toward him. Soren madly tried to beat his stubby little wings. *Useless! He thought, I am dead. A dead owlet. Three weeks out of the shell and my life ends!*

Suddenly, something began to soften his fall — a pocket of breeze? A cushion of wind? A downy fluff of air lacing through his unsightly patches of fuzz? What was it? Time slowed. His short life flowed by him — every second of it from his very first memory. . . .

CHAPTER ONE

A Nest Remembered

Noctus, can you spare a bit more down, darling? I think our third little one is about to arrive. That egg is beginning to crack."

"Not again!" sighed Kludd.

"What do you mean, Kludd, not again? Don't you want another little brother?" his father said. There was an edge to his voice.

"Or sister?" His mother sighed the low soft whistle Barn Owls sometimes used.

"I'd like a sister," Soren peeped up.

"You just hatched out two weeks ago." Kludd turned to Soren, his younger brother. "What do you know about sisters?"

Maybe, Soren thought to himself, *they would be better than brothers.* Kludd seemed to have resented him since the moment he had first hatched.

"You really wouldn't want them arriving just when you're about to begin branching," Kludd said dully. Branching was the first step, literally, toward flight. The young owlets would begin by hopping from branch to branch and flapping their wings.

"Now, now, Kludd!" his father admonished. "Don't be impatient. There'll be time for branching. Remember, you won't have your flight feathers for at least another month or more."

Soren was just about to ask what a month was when he heard a *crack*. The owl family all seemed to freeze. To any other forest creature the sound would have been imperceptible. But Barn Owls were blessed with extraordinary hearing.

"It's coming!" Soren's mother gasped. "I'm so excited." She sighed again and looked rapturously at the pure white egg as it rocked back and forth. A tiny hole appeared and from it protruded a small spur.

"Its egg tooth, by Glaux!" Soren's father exclaimed.

"Mine was bigger wasn't it, Da?" Kludd shoved Soren aside for a better look, but Soren crept back up under his father's wing.

"Oh, I don't know, son. But isn't it a pretty, glistening little point. Always gives me a thrill. Such a tiny little thing pecking its way into the big wide world. Ah! Bless my gizzard, the wonder of it all."

It did indeed seem a wonder. Soren stared at the hole

that now began to split into two or three cracks. The egg shuddered slightly and the cracks grew longer and wider. He had done this himself just two weeks ago. This *was* exciting.

"What happened to my egg tooth, Mum?"

"It dropped off, stupid," Kludd said.

"Oh," Soren said quietly. His parents were so absorbed in the hatching that they didn't reprimand Kludd for his rudeness.

"Where's Mrs. P.? Mrs. P.?" his mother said urgently.

"Right here, ma'am." Mrs. Plithiver, the old blind snake who had been with the owl family for years and years, slithered into the hollow. Blind snakes, born without eyes, served as nest-maids and were kept by many owls to make sure the nests were clean and free of maggots and various insects that found their way into the hollows.

"Mrs. P., no maggots or vermin in that corner where Noctus put in fresh down."

"'Course not, ma'am. Now, how many broods of owlets have I been through with you?"

"Oh, sorry, Mrs. P. How could I have ever doubted you? I'm always nervous at the hatching. Each one is just like the first time. I never get used to it."

"Don't you apologize, ma'am. You think any other birds would care two whits if their nest was clean? The stories

I've heard about seagulls! Oh, my goodness! Well, I won't even go into it."

Blind snakes prided themselves on working for owls, whom they considered the noblest of birds. Meticulous, the blind snakes had great disdain for other birds that they felt were less clean due to their unfortunate digestive processes that caused them to eliminate only sloppy wet droppings instead of nice neat bundles — the pellets that owls yarped, or spit up. Although owls did digest the soft parts of their food in a manner similar to other birds, and indeed passed it in a liquid form, for some reason they were never associated with these lesser digestive processes. All the fur and bones and tiny teeth of their prey, like mice, that could not be digested in the ordinary way were pressed into little pellets just the shape and size of the owl's gizzard. Several hours after eating, the owls would yarp them up. "Wet poopers" is how many nest-maid snakes referred to other birds. Of course, Mrs. Plithiver was much too proper to use such coarse language.

"Mum!" Soren gasped. "Look at that." The nest suddenly seemed to reverberate with a huge cracking sound. Again, only huge to the ear slits of Barn Owls. Now the egg split. A pale slimy blob flopped out.

"It's a girl!" A long *shree* call streamed from his mother's throat. It was the shree of pure happiness. "Adorable!" Soren's mother sighed.

"Enchanting!" said Soren's father.

Kludd yawned and Soren stared dumbfounded at the wet naked thing with its huge bulging eyes sealed tightly shut.

"What's wrong with her head, Mum?" Soren asked.

"Nothing, dear. Chicks just have very large heads. It takes a while for their bodies to catch up."

"Not to mention their brains," Kludd muttered.

"So they can't hold their heads up right away," said his mother. "You were the same way."

"What shall we call the little dear?" Soren's father asked.

"Eglantine," Soren's mother replied immediately. "I have always wanted a little Eglantine."

"Oooh! Mum, I love that name," Soren said. He softly repeated the name. Then he tipped toward the little pulsing mass of white. "Eglantine," he whispered softly, and he thought he saw one little sealed eye open just a slit and a tiny voice seemed to say *"hi."* Soren loved his little sister immediately.

One second, Eglantine had been this quivering little wet blob, and then, minutes later, it seemed as if she had turned into a fluffy white ball of down. She grew stronger quickly, or so it appeared to Soren. His parents assured him that he, too, had done exactly the same. That evening it was time for her First Insect ceremony. Her eyes were fully open and she was bawling with hunger. Eglantine could hardly make it through her father's "Welcome to Tyto" speech.

"Little Eglantine, welcome to the Forest of Tyto, forest of the Barn Owls, or Tyto alba, as we are more formally known. Once upon a time, long long ago, we did indeed live in barns. But now, we and other Tyto cousins live in this forest kingdom known as Tyto. We are rare indeed and we are perhaps the smallest of all the owl kingdoms. Although, in truth, it has been a long long time since we had a king. Someday when you grow up, when you enter your second year, you, too, will fly out from this hollow and find one of your own in which to live with a mate."

This was the part of the speech that amazed and disturbed Soren. He simply could not imagine growing up and having a nest of his own. How could he be separated from his parents? And yet there was this urge to fly, even now with his stubby little wings that lacked even the smallest sign of true flight feathers. "And now," Soren's father continued, "it is time for your First Insect ceremony." He turned to Soren's mother. "Marella, my dear, can you bring forward the cricket?"

Soren's mother stepped up. In her beak she held one of the summer's last crickets. "Eat up, young'un! Headfirst. Yes, down the beak. Yes, always headfirst — that's the proper way, be it cricket, mouse, or vole."

"Mmmm," sighed Soren's father as he watched his daughter swallow the cricket. "Dizzy in the gizzy, ain't it so?!"

Kludd blinked and yawned. Sometimes his parents really embarrassed him, especially his da with his stupid jokes. "Wit of the wood!" muttered Kludd.

That dawn, after the owls had settled down, Soren was still so excited by his little sister's arrival that he could not sleep. His parents had retired to the ledge above him where they slept, but he could hear their voices threading through the dim morning light that filtered into the hollow.

"Oh, Noctus, it is very strange — another owlet disappeared?"

"Yes, my dear, I'm afraid so."

"How many is that now in the last few days?"

"Fifteen missing, I believe."

"That is many more than can be accounted for by raccoons."

"Yes," Noctus replied grimly. "And there is something else."

"What?" his wife replied in a lower wavering hoot.

"Eggs."

"Eggs?"

"Eggs have disappeared."

"Eggs from a nest?"

"Yes, I'm afraid so."

"No!" Marella Alba gasped. "I have never heard of such a thing. It's unspeakable."

"I thought I must tell you in case we are blessed with another brood."

"Oh, great Glaux," his mother gasped. Soren's eyes blinked wide. He had never heard his mother swear before. "But we so seldom leave the nest during broody times. Whoever it is must watch us." She paused. "Watch us constantly."

"Whoever it is can fly or climb," Noctus Alba said darkly.

Soren felt a sense of dread seep into the hollow. How thankful he was that Eglantine had not been snatched while just an egg. He vowed he would never leave her alone.

It seemed to Soren that as soon as Eglantine ate her first insect she never stopped eating. His mother and father assured him that he had been the same. "And you still are, Soren! And it's almost time for your first Fur-on-Meat ceremony!"

That was what life was like those first weeks in the

nest — one ceremony after another. Each, it seemed in some way or another, led to the truly biggest, perhaps the most solemn yet joyous moment in a young owl's life: First Flight.

"Fur!" whispered Soren. He couldn't quite imagine what it was like. What it would feel like slipping down his throat. His mother always stripped off all the fur from the meat and then tore out the bones before offering the little tidbits of fresh mouse or squirrel to Soren. Kludd was almost ready for his First Bones ceremony when he would be allowed to eat "the whole bit" as Soren's father said. And it was just before First Bones that a young owl began branching. And just after that, it would begin its first real flight under the watchful eyes of its parents.

"Hop! Hop! That's it, Kludd! Now, up with the wings just as you begin the hop to that next branch. And remember, you are just branching now. No flying. And even after your first flight lessons, no flying by yourself until Mum and I say so."

"Yes, Da!" Kludd said in a bored voice. Then he muttered, "How many times have I heard this lecture!"

Soren had heard it many many times, too, even though he was nowhere near branching. The worst thing a young owl could do was to try to fly before it was ready. And, of course, young owls usually did this when their parents were out hunting. It was so tempting to try one's newly fledged wings, but it would most likely end in a disastrous crash, leaving the little owlet nestless, perhaps badly injured, and on the ground exposed to dangerous predators. The lecture was brief this time, and the branching lesson resumed.

"Crisply! Crisply, boy! Keep the noise down. Owls are silent fliers."

"But I'm not flying yet, Da! As you keep reminding me constantly! What's it matter if I'm noisy now when I'm just branching?"

"Bad habit! Bad habit! Leads to noisy flight. Hard to outgrow noise habits started in branching."

"Oh, bother!"

"Oh, I'll bother you!" Noctus exploded, and gave his son a cuff on the head that nearly tipped him over. Soren had to admit that Kludd didn't even whimper but just picked himself up and gave his da a glaring look and resumed hopping — slightly less noisily than before.

There was a series of soft short hisses from Mrs. Plithiver. "Difficult one, that one! My! My! Glad your mum's not here to see this. Eglantine!" Mrs. Plithiver called out suddenly. Even though she was blind she seemed to know exactly what the young owlets were doing at any given moment. She now heard the crunch of a nest bug in

Eglantine's beak. "Put that nest bug down. Owls do not eat nest bugs. That's what house snakes do. If you keep it up, you'll just grow fat and squishy and won't be prepared for your First Meat ceremony, and then no First Fur, and then no First Bones, and then no, well, you know what. Now your mum is just out looking for a nice chubby vole with soft fur for Soren's First Fur ceremony. And she might even find a nice wriggly little centipede for you."

"Ooh, they're so much fun to eat!" Soren exclaimed. "All their little legs pittering down your gullet."

"Oh, Soren, tell me that story about the first time you ate a centipede," Eglantine begged.

Mrs. Plithiver sighed softly. It was so sweet! Eglantine hung on every word of Soren's. True sisterly love, and Soren loved her right back. She wasn't sure what exactly had happened with their older brother, Kludd. There was always one difficult one in a brood, but Kludd was more than just difficult. *There was something . . . something . . .* Mrs. Plithiver thought hard. Just something missing with Kludd. Something rather unnatural, un-owlish.

"Sing the centipede song, Soren! Sing it!"

Soren opened his beak wide and began to sing:

> *What gives a wriggle*
> *And makes you giggle*

When you eat 'em?
Whose weensy little feet
Make my heart really beat?
Why, it's those little creepy crawlies
That make me feel so jolly.

For the darling centipede
My favorite buggy feed
I always want some more.
That's the insect I adore
More than beetles, more than crickets,
Which at times give me the hiccups.
I crave only to feed
On a juicy centipede
And I shall be happy forevermore.

Just as Soren finished the song, his mother flew into the hollow and dropped a vole at her feet. "A nice fat one, my dear. Enough for your First Fur ceremony and Kludd's First Bones."

"I want my own!" Kludd said.

"Nonsense, dear, you could never eat a whole vole."

"Whole vole!" squeaked Eglantine. "Oh, Mum, it rhymes. I love rhymes."

"I want one all for myself," Kludd persisted.

"Now, look here, Kludd." Marella fixed her son in a dark steady gaze. "We do not waste food around here. This is a very large vole. There is enough for you to have your First Bones ceremony, Soren to have his First Fur ceremony, and Eglantine to have her First Meat."

"Meat! I get to eat meat!" Eglantine gave a little hop of excitement. She seemed to have forgotten all about the joys of centipedes.

"And so, Kludd, when you want a vole all of your own, you can just go out and hunt it for yourself! I spent most of the night tracking down this one. Food is scarce in Tyto this time of year. I'm exhausted." A huge orange moon sailed in the autumn sky. It seemed to hover just above the great fir tree where Soren and his family lived, and it cast a soft glow in through the opening of the hollow. It was indeed a perfect night for the ceremonies that these owls loved and that marked their growth and the passage of time.

And so that night, just before the dawn, the three little owlets had their First Meat, First Fur, and First Bone ceremonies. And Kludd yarped his first real pellet. It was the exact shape of his gizzard, which had pressed it into the tight little bundle of bones and fur. "Oh, that's a fine pellet, son," Kludd's father said.

"Yes, indeed," his mother agreed. "Quite admirable."

And Kludd, for once, seemed satisfied. And Mrs. Plithiver thought privately to herself how no bird could be really bad that had such a noble digestive system.

That night, from the time the big orange moon began to slip down in the sky until the first gray streaks of the new dawn, Noctus Alba told the stories that owls had loved to hear from the time of Glaux. Glaux was the most ancient order of owls from which all other owls descended.

So his father began:

"Once upon a very long time ago, in the time of Glaux, there was an order of knightly owls, from a kingdom called Ga'Hoole, who would rise each night into the blackness and perform noble deeds. They spoke no words but true ones, their purpose was to right all wrongs, to make strong the weak, mend the broken, vanquish the proud, and make powerless those who abused the frail. With hearts sublime they would take flight —"

Kludd yawned. "Is this a true story or what, Da?"

"It's a legend, Kludd," his father answered.

"But is it true?" Kludd whined. "I only like true stories."

"A legend, Kludd, is a story that you begin to feel in your gizzard and then over time it becomes true in your heart. And perhaps makes you become a better owl."

CHAPTER TWO
A Life Worth Two Pellets

True in your heart! Those words in the deep throaty hoot of his father were perhaps the last thing Soren remembered before he landed with a soft thud on a pile of moss. Shaking himself and feeling a bit dazed, he tried to stand up. Nothing seemed broken. But how had this happened? He certainly had not tried flying while his parents were out hunting. Good Glaux. He hadn't even tried branching yet. He was still far from "flight readiness" as his mum called it. So how had this happened? All he knew was, one moment he was near the edge of the hollow, peering out, looking for his mum and da to come home from hunting, and the next minute he was tumbling through the air.

Soren tipped his head up. The fir tree was so tall, and he knew that their hollow was near the very top. What had his father said — ninety feet, one hundred feet? But numbers had no meaning for Soren. Not only could he not fly, he couldn't count, either. Didn't really know his numbers. But there was one thing that he did know: He was in trouble — deep, frightening, horrifying trouble. The boring lectures that Kludd had complained about came back to him. The weight of the terrible truth now pressed upon him in the darkness of the forest — those grim words, "an owlet that is separated from its parents before it has learned to fly and hunt cannot survive."

And Soren's parents were gone, gone on a long hunting flight. There had not been many since Eglantine had hatched out. But they needed more food, for winter was coming. So right now Soren was completely alone. He could not imagine being more completely alone as he gazed up at the tree that seemed to vanish into the clouds. He sighed and muttered, "So alone, so alone."

And yet, deep inside him something flickered like a tiny smoldering spark of hope. When he had fallen, he must have done something with his nearly bald wings that "had captured the air" as his father would say. He tried now to recall that feeling. For a brief instant, falling had actually felt wonderful. Could he perhaps recapture that air? He tried to lift his wings and flutter them slightly. Nothing. His wings felt cold and bare in the crisp autumn breeze. He looked at the tree again. Could he climb, using his talons and beak? He had to do something fast or he would become some creature's next meal — a rat, a raccoon. Soren felt faint at the very thought of a raccoon. He had seen them from the nest — bushy, masked, horrible creatures with sharp teeth. He must listen carefully. He must turn and tip his head as his parents had taught him. His parents could listen so carefully that, from high above in their tree hollow, they could hear the heartbeat of a mouse on the forest floor below. Surely he should be able to hear a raccoon. He cocked his head and nearly jumped. He did hear a sound. It was a small, raspy, familiar voice from high up in the fir tree. "Soren! Soren!" it called from the hollow where his brother and sister still nestled in the fluffy pure white down that their parents had plucked from beneath their flight feathers. But it was neither Kludd nor Eglantine.

"Mrs. Plithiver!" Soren cried.

"Soren . . . are you . . . are you alive? Oh, dear, of course you are if you can say my name. How stupid of me. Are you well? Did you break anything?"

"I don't think so, but how will I ever get back up there?"

"Oh, dear! Oh, dear," Mrs. Plithiver moaned. She was not much good in a crisis. One could not expect such things of nest-maids, Soren supposed.

"How long until Mum and Da get home?" Soren called up.

"Oh, it could be a long while, dearie."

Soren had hop-stepped to the roots of the tree that ran above the ground like gnarled talons. He could now see Mrs. Plithiver, her small head with its glistening rosy scales hovering over the edge of the hollow. Where Mrs. Plithiver's eyes should have been there were two small indentations. "This is simply beyond me." She sighed.

"Is Kludd awake? Maybe he could help me."

There was a long pause before Mrs. Plithiver answered weakly, "Well, perhaps." She sounded hesitant. Soren could hear her now, nudging Kludd. "Don't be grumpy, Kludd. Your brother has . . . has . . . taken a tumble, as it were."

Soren heard his brother yawn. "Oh, my." Kludd sighed and didn't sound especially upset, Soren thought. Soon the large head of his big brother peered over the edge of the hollow. His white heart-shaped face with the immense dark eyes peered down on Soren. "I say," Kludd drawled. "You've got yourself in a terrible fix."

"I know, Kludd. Can't you help? You know more about flying than I do. Can't you teach me?"

"Me teach you? I wouldn't know where to begin. Have you gone yoicks?" He laughed. "Stark-raving yoicks. Me teach you?" He laughed again. There was a sneer embedded deep within the laugh.

"I'm not yoicks. But you're always telling me how

much you know, Kludd." This was certainly the truth. Kludd had been bragging about his superiority ever since Soren had hatched out. *He* should get the favorite spot in the hollow because *he* was already losing his downy fluff in preparation for his flight feathers and therefore would be colder. *He* deserved the largest hunks of mouse meat because *he*, after all, was on the brink of flying. "You've already had your First Flight ceremony. Tell me how to fly, Kludd."

"One cannot tell another how to fly. It's a feeling, and besides, it is really a job for Mum and Da. It would be very impertinent of me to usurp their position."

Soren had no idea what "usurp" meant. Kludd often used big words to impress him.

"What are you talking about? Usurp?" Sounded like "yarp" to Soren. But what would yarping have to do with teaching him to fly? Time was running out. The light was leaking out of the day's end and the evening shadows were falling. The raccoons would soon be out.

"I can't do it, Soren," Kludd replied in a very serious voice. "It would be extremely improper for a young owlet like myself to assume this role in your life."

"My life isn't going to be worth two pellets if you don't do something. Don't you think it is improper for you to let me die? What will Mum and Da say to that?"

"I think they will understand completely."

Great Glaux! Understand completely! He had to be yoicks. Soren was simply too dumbfounded. He could not say another word.

"I'm going to get help, Soren. I'll go to Hilda's," he heard Mrs. P. rasp. Hilda was another nest-maid snake for an owl family in a tree near the banks of the river.

"I wouldn't if I were you, P." Kludd's voice was ominous. It made Soren's gizzard absolutely quiver.

"Don't call me P. That's so rude."

"That's the last thing you have to worry about P. — me being rude."

Soren blinked.

"I'm going, Kludd. You can't stop me," Mrs. Plithiver said firmly.

"Can't I?"

Soren heard a rustling sound above. *Good Glaux, what was happening?*

"Mrs. Plithiver?" Only silence now. "Mrs. Plithiver?" Soren called again. Maybe she had gone to Hilda's. He could only hope, and wait.

It was nearly dark now and a chill wind rose up. There was no sign of Mrs. Plithiver returning. "First teeth" — isn't that what Da always called these early cold winds? — the first teeth of winter. The very words made poor Soren shudder. When his father had first used this expression, Soren had no idea what "teeth" even were. His father explained that they were something that owls didn't have, but most other animals did. They were for tearing and chewing food.

"Does Mrs. Plithiver have them?" asked Soren. Mrs. Plithiver had gasped in disgust.

His mother said, "Of course not, dear."

"Well, what are they exactly?" Soren had asked.

"Hmm," said his mother as she thought a moment. "Just imagine a mouth full of beaks — yes, very sharp beaks."

"That sounds very scary."

"Yes, it can be," his mother replied. "That is why you do not want to fall out of the hollow or try to fly before you're ready, because raccoons have very sharp teeth."

"You see," his father broke in, "we have no need for such things as teeth. Our gizzards take care of all that chewing business. I find it rather revolting, the notion of actually chewing something in one's mouth."

"They say it adds flavor, darling," his mother added.

"I get flavor, plenty of flavor, in my gizzard. Where do you think that old expression 'I know it in my gizzard' comes from? Or 'I have a feeling in my gizzard,' Marella?"

"Noctus, I'm not sure if that is the same thing as flavor."

"That mouse we had for dinner last night — I can tell

you from my gizzard exactly where he had been of late. He had been feasting on the sweet grass of the meadow mixed with the nooties from that little Ga'Hoole tree that grows down by the stream. Great Glaux! I don't need teeth to taste."

Oh, dear, thought Soren, he might never hear this gentle bickering between his parents again. A centipede pittered by and Soren did not even care. Darkness gathered. The black of the night grew deeper and from down on the ground he could barely see the stars. This perhaps was the worst. He could not see sky through the thickness of the trees. How much he missed the hollow. From their nest, there was always a little piece of the sky to watch. At night, it sparkled with stars or raced with clouds. In the daytime, there was often a lovely patch of blue, and sometimes toward evening, before twilight, the clouds turned bright orange or pink. There was an odd smell down here on the ground — damp and moldy. The wind sighed through the branches above, through the leaves and the needles of the forest trees, but down on the ground . . . well, the wind didn't seem to even touch the ground. There was a terrible stillness. It was the stillness of a windless place. This was no place for an owl to be. Everything was different.

If his feathers had been even half-fledged, he could

have plumped them up and the downy fluff beneath the flight feathers would have kept him warm. He supposed he could try calling for Eglantine. But what use would she be? She was so young. Besides, if he called out, wouldn't that alert other creatures in the forest that he was here? Creatures with teeth!

He guessed his life wasn't worth two pellets. But even worthless, he still missed his parents. He missed them so much that the missing felt sharp. Yes, he did feel something in his gizzard as sharp as a tooth.

CHAPTER THREE
Snatched!

Soren was dreaming of teeth and of the heartbeats of mice when he heard the first soft rustlings overhead. "Mum! Da!" he cried out in his half sleep. He would forever regret calling out those two words, for suddenly, the night was ripped with a shrill screech, and Soren felt talons wrap around him. Now he was being lifted. And they were flying fast, faster than he could think, faster than he could ever imagine. His parents never flew this fast. He had watched them when they took off or came back from the hollow. They glided slowly and rose in beautiful lazy spirals into the night. But now, underneath, the earth raced by. Slivers of air blistered his skin. The moon rolled out from behind thick clouds and bleached the world with an eerie whiteness. He scoured the landscape below for the tree that had been his home. But the trees blurred into clumps, and then the forest of the Kingdom of Tyto seemed to grow smaller and smaller and dimmer and dimmer in the night, until Soren could not stand to look down anymore. So he dared to look up.

There was a great bushiness of feathers on the owl's legs. His eyes continued upward. This was a huge owl — or was it even an owl? Atop this creature's head, over each eye, were two tufts of feathers that looked like an extra set of wings. Just as Soren was thinking this was the strangest owl he had ever seen, the owl blinked and looked down. Yellow eyes! He had never seen such eyes. His own parents and his brother and sister all had dark, almost black eyes. His parents' friends who occasionally flew by had brown-ish eyes, perhaps some with a tinge of tawny gold. But yellow eyes? This was wrong. Very wrong!

"Surprised!" The owl blinked, but Soren could not speak. So the owl continued. "Yes, you see, that's the problem with the Kingdom of Tyto — you never see any other kind of owl but your own kind — lowly, undistinguished Barn Owls."

"That's not true," said Soren.

"You dare contradict me!" screeched the owl.

"I've seen Grass Owls and Masked Owls. I've seen Bay Owls and Sooty Owls. Some of my parents' very best friends are Grass Owls."

"Stupid! They're all Tytos," the owl barked at him.

Stupid? Grown-ups weren't supposed to speak this way — not to young owls, not to chicks. It was mean. Soren decided he should be quiet. He would stop looking up.

"We might have a haggard here," he heard the owl say. Soren turned his head slightly to see who the owl was speaking to.

"Oh, great Glaux! One wonders if it is worth the effort." This owl's eyes seemed more brown than yellow and his feathers were spattered with splotches of white and gray and brown.

"Oh, I think it is always worth the effort, Grimble. And don't let Spoorn hear you talking that way. You'll get a demerit and then we'll all be forced to attend another one of her interminable lectures on attitude."

This owl looked different as well. Not nearly as big as the other owl and his voice made a soft *tingg-tingg* sound. It was at least a minute before Soren noticed that this owl was also carrying something in his talons. It was a creature of some sort and it looked rather owlish, but it was so small, hardly larger than a mouse. Then it blinked its eyes. Yellow! Soren resisted the urge to yarp. "Don't say a word!" the small owl said in a squeaky whisper. "Wait."

Wait for what? Soren wondered. But soon he felt the night stir with the beating of other wings. More owls fell in beside them. Each one carried an owlet in its talons.

Then there was a low hum from the owl that gripped Soren. Gradually, the other owls flanking them joined in. Soon the air thrummed with a strange music. "It's their hymn," whispered the tiny owl. "It gets louder. That's when we can talk."

Soren listened to the words of the hymn.

> *Hail to St. Aegolius*
> *Our Alma Mater.*
> *Hail, our song we raise in praise of thee*
> *Long in the memory of every loyal owl*
> *Thy splendid banner emblazoned be.*
>
> *Now to thy golden talons*
> *Homage we're bringing.*
> *Guiding symbol of our hopes and fears*
> *Hark to the cries of eternal praises ringing*
> *Long may we triumph in the coming years.*

The tiny owl began to speak as the voices swelled in the black of the night. "My first words of advice are to listen rather than speak. You've already got yourself marked as a wild owl, a haggard."

"Who are you? What are you? Why do you have yellow eyes?"

"You see what I mean! That is the last thing that you should worry about." The tiny owl sighed softly. "But I'll tell you. I am an Elf Owl. My name is Gylfie."

"I've never seen one in Tyto."

"We live in the high desert kingdom of Kuneer."

"Do you ever grow any bigger?"

"No. This is it."

"But you're so small and you've got all of your feathers, or almost."

"Yes, this is the worst part. I was within a week or so of flying when I got snatched."

"But how old are you?"

"Twenty nights."

"Twenty nights!" Soren exclaimed. "How can you fly that young?"

"Elf Owls are able to fly by twenty-seven or thirty nights."

"How much is sixty-six nights?" Soren asked.

"A lot."

"I'm a Barn Owl and we can't fly for sixty-six nights. But what happened to you? How did you get snatched?"

Gylfie did not answer right away. Then slowly, "What is the ONE thing that your parents always tell you not to do?"

"Fly before you're ready?" Soren said.

"I tried and I fell."

"But I don't understand. It would have been only a week, you said." Soren, of course, wasn't sure how long a week was or how long twenty-seven nights were, but it all sounded shorter than sixty-six.

"I was impatient. I was well on my way to growing feathers but had grown no patience." Gylfie paused again. "But what about yourself? You must have tried it, too."

"No. I don't really know what happened. I just fell out of the nest." But the second Soren said those words he felt a weird queasiness. He almost knew. He just couldn't quite remember, but he almost knew how it had happened, and he felt a mixture of dread and shame creep through him. He felt something terrible deep in his gizzard.

CHAPTER FOUR

St. Aegolius Academy for Orphaned Owls

The owls began to bank in steep turns as they circled downward. Soren blinked and looked down. There was not a tree, not a stream, not a meadow. Instead, immense rock needles bristled up, and cutting through them were deep stone ravines and jagged canyons. This could not be Tyto. That was all that Soren could think.

Down, down, down they plunged in tighter and tighter circles, until they alighted on the stony floor of a deep, narrow canyon. And, although Soren could indeed see the sky from which they had just plunged, it seemed farther away than ever. Above, there was the sound of wind, distant yet shrill as it whistled across the upper reaches of this harsh stone world. Then, piercing through the shriek of the wind, came a voice even louder and sharper.

"Welcome, owlets. Welcome to St. Aegolius. This is

your new home. It is here that you will find truth and purpose. Yes, that is our motto. When Truth Is Found, Purpose Is Revealed."

The immense, ragged Great Horned Owl fixed them in her yellow gaze. The tufts above her eyes swooped up. The shoulder feathers on her left wing had separated, revealing an unsightly patch of skin with a jagged white scar. She was perched on a rock outcropping in the granite ravine where they had been brought. "I am Skench, Ablah General of St. Aegolius. My job is to teach you the Truth. We discourage questions here as we feel they often distract from the Truth." Soren found this very confusing. He had always asked questions, ever since he had hatched out.

Skench, the Ablah General, was continuing her speech. "You are orphans now." The words shocked Soren. He was not an orphan! He had a mum and da, perhaps not here, but out there somewhere. Orphan meant your parents were dead. How dare this Skench, the Ablah blah blah blah, or whatever she called herself, say he was an orphan!

"We have rescued you. It is here at St. Aggie's that you shall find everything that you need to become humble, plain servants of a higher good."

This was the most outrageous thing Soren had ever heard. He hadn't been rescued, he had been snatched away. If he had been rescued, these owls would have flown

31

up and dropped him back in his family's nest. And what exactly was a higher good?

"There are many ways in which one can serve the higher good, and it is our job to find out which best suits you and to discover what your special talents are." Skench narrowed her eyes until they were gleaming amber slits in her feathery face. "I am sure that each and every one of you has something special."

At that very moment, there was a chorus of hoots, and many owl voices were raised in song.

> To find one's special quality
> One must lead a life of deep humility.
> To serve in this way
> Never question but obey
> Is the blessing of St. Aggie's charity.

At the conclusion of the short song, Skench, the Ablah General, swooped down from her stone perch. She fixed them all in the glare of her eyes. "You are embarking on an exciting adventure, little orphans. After I have dismissed you, you shall be led to one of four glaucidiums, where two things shall occur. You shall receive your number designation. And you shall also receive your first lesson in the proper manner in which to sleep and shall be inducted into the march of sleep. These are the first steps toward the Specialness ceremony."

What in the world was this owl talking about? Soren wondered. Number designation? What was a glaucidium, and since when did an owl have to be taught to sleep? And a sleep march? What was that? And it was still night. What owl slept at night? But before he could really ponder these questions, he felt himself being gently shoved into a line, a separate line from the little Elf Owl called Gylfie. He turned his head nearly completely around to search for Gylfie and caught sight of her. He raised a stubby wing to wave but Gylfie did not see him. He saw her marching ahead with her eyes looking straight forward.

The line Soren was in wound its way through a series of deep gorges. It was like a stone maze of tangled trails through the gaps and canyons and notches of this place called St. Aegolius Academy for Orphaned Owls. Soren had the unsettling feeling that he might never see the little Elf Owl again, and even worse, it would be impossible to ever find one's way out of these stone boxes into the forest world of Tyto, with its immense trees and sparkling streams.

They finally came to stop in a circular stone pit. A white owl with very thick feathers waddled toward them and blinked. Her eyes had a soft yellow glow.

"I am Finny, your pit guardian." And then she giggled softly. "Some have been known to call me their pit angel." She gazed sweetly at them. "I would love it if you would all call me Auntie."

Auntie? Soren wondered. *Why would I ever call her Auntie?* But he remembered not to ask.

"I must, of course, call you by your number designation, which you shall shortly be told," said Finny.

"Oh, goody!" A little Spotted Owl standing next to Soren hopped up and down.

This time, Soren remembered too late that questions were discouraged. "Why do you want a number instead of your name?"

"Hortense! You wouldn't like that name, either," the Spotted Owl whispered. "Now, shush. Remember, no questions."

"You shall, of course," Finny continued, "if you are good humble owlets and learn the lessons of humility and obedience, earn your Specialness rank and then receive your true name."

But my true name is Soren. It is the name my parents gave me. The words pounded in Soren's head and even his gizzard seemed to tremble in protest.

"Now, let's line up for our Number ceremony, and I have a tempting little snack here for you."

There were perhaps twenty owls in Soren's group and Soren was toward the middle of the line. He watched as the white owl, Auntie or Finny, whom Hortense had informed him was a Snowy Owl, dropped a piece of fur-stripped mouse meat on the stone before each owl in turn and then said, "Why, you're number 12-6. What a nice number that is, dearie."

Every number was either "nice," or "dear," or "darling." Finny bent her head solicitously and often gave a friendly little pat to the owlet just "numbered." She was full of quips and little jokes. Soren was just beginning to feel that things perhaps could be worse, and he hoped that Gylfie had such a nice owl for a pit guardian, when the huge fierce owl with the tufts over each eye, the very one who had snatched him and called him stupid, alighted down next to Finny. Soren felt a cold dread steal over his gizzard as he saw the owl look directly at him and then dip his head and whisper something into Finny's ear. Finny nodded and looked at him blandly. They were talking about him. Soren was sure. He could barely move his talons forward on the hard stone toward Finny. His turn was coming up soon. Only four more owls before he would be "numbered."

"Hello, sweetness," Finny cooed as Soren stepped forward. "I have a very special number for you!" Soren was silent. Finny continued, "Don't you want to know what it is?" *This is a trick. Questions are discouraged. I'm not supposed to ask.* And that was exactly what Soren said.

"I'm not supposed to ask." The soft yellow glow streamed from Finny's eyes. Soren felt a moment's confusion. Then Finny leaned forward and whispered to him. "You know, dear, I'm not as strict as some. So please, if you really really need to ask a question, just go ahead. But remember to keep your voice down. And here, dear, is a little extra piece of mouse. And your number . . ." She sighed and her entire white face seemed to glow with the yellow light. "My favorite — 12-1. Isn't it sublime! It's a very special number, and I am sure that you will discover your own very specialness as an owl."

"Thank you," Soren said, still slightly mystified but relieved that the fierce owl had apparently not told Finny anything bad about him.

"Thank you, what?" Finny giggled. "See? I get to ask questions, too, sometimes."

"Thank you, Finny?"

Finny inclined her head toward him again. There was a slight glare in the yellow glow. "Again," she whispered softly. "Again . . . now, look me in the eyes." Soren looked into the yellow light.

"Thank you, Auntie."

36

"Yes, dear. I'm just an old broody. Love being called Auntie."

Soren did not know what a broody was, but he took the mouse meat and followed the owl who had been in front of him into the glaucidium. Two large, ragged brown owls escorted the entire group. The glaucidium was a deep box canyon, the floor of which was covered with sleeping owlets. Moonlight streamed down directly on them, silvering their feathers.

"Fall in, you two!" barked a voice from high up in a rocky crevice.

"You!" A plump owl stepped up to Soren. Indeed, Soren's heart quickened at first, for it was another Barn Owl just like his own family. There was the white heart-shaped face and the familiar dark eyes. And yet, although the color of these eyes was identical to his own and those of his family, he found the owl's gaze frightening.

"Back row, and prepare to assume the sleeping position." These instructions were delivered in the throaty rasp common to Barn Owls, but Soren found nothing comforting in the familiar.

The two owls who had escorted the newly arrived orphans spoke to them next. They were Long Eared Owls and had tufts that poked straight up over their eyes and twitched. Soren found this especially unnerving. They each alternated speaking in short deep *whoos*. The *whoos* were even more disturbing than the barks of Skench earlier, for the sound seemed to coil into Soren's very breast and thrum with a terrible *clang*.

"I am Jatt," said the first owl. "I was once a number. But now I have earned my new name."

"*Whhh —*" Soren snapped off the word.

"I see a question forming on your disgusting beak, number 12-1!" The *whoo* thrummed so deep within Soren's breast that he thought his heart might burst.

"Let me make this perrr-fectly clear." The thrumming of the owl's sound was almost unbearable. "At St. Aggie's such words beginning with the *whh* sound are not to be spoken. Such words are question words, a habit of mental luxury and indulgence. Questions might fatten the imagination, but they starve the owlish instincts of hardiness, patience, humility, and self-denial. We are not here to pamper you by allowing an orgy of *wwwhh* words, question words. They are dirty words, swear words punishable by the most severe means at our disposal." Jatt blinked and cast his gaze on Soren's wings. "We are here to make true owls out of you. And someday you will thank us for it."

Soren thought he was going to faint with fear. These owls were so different from Finny. *Auntie!* He silently corrected himself. Jatt had resumed speaking in his normal *whoo.* "Now my cousin shall address you."

It was an identical voice. "I am Jutt. I, too, was once a number but have earned my new name. You are now in the sleeping position. Standing tall, head up, beak tipped to the moon. You see in this glaucidium hundreds of owlets. They have all learned to sleep in this manner. You, too, shall learn."

Soren looked around, desperately searching for Gylfie, but all he saw was Hortense, or number 12-8. She had assumed the perfect sleeping position. He could tell by the stillness of her head that she was sound asleep under the glare of a full moon. Soren spotted a stone arch that connected to what he thought was another glaucidium. A mass of owls seemed to be marching. Their beaks were bobbing open and shut but Soren could not hear what they were saying.

Jatt now spoke again. "It is strictly forbidden to sleep with the head tucked under the wings, dipped toward the breast, or in the manner that many of you young owls are accustomed, which is the semi-twist position in which the head rests on the back." Soren felt at least seven *wh* sounds die mutely in his throat. "Incorrect sleeping posture is also punishable, using our most severe methods."

"Sleep correction monitors patrol the glaucidium, making their rounds at regular intervals," Jutt continued.

Now it was Jatt's turn again. Their timing seemed perfect. Soren felt they had given this speech many times. "Also, at regular intervals, you shall hear the alarm. At the sound, all owlets in the glaucidium are required to begin the sleep march."

"During the sleep march," Jutt resumed, "you march, repeating your old name over and over and over again. When the second alarm sounds, you halt where you are. Repeat your number designation one time, and one time only, and assume the sleep position once more."

Both owls next spoke at once in an awesome thrum. "Now, sleep!"

Soren tried to sleep. He really did try. Maybe Finny, he meant *Auntie*, would believe him. But there was just something in his gizzard, a little twinge, that seemed to make sleep impossible. It was almost as if the shine of the full moon that sprayed its light over half the glaucidium became a sharp silver needle stabbing through his skull and going straight to his gizzard. Perhaps he had a very sensitive gizzard like his da. But in this case he wasn't "tasting" the sweet grass the meadow mouse had feasted on. He was tasting dread.

Soren was not sure how long it was before the alarm sounded but it was soon time for his first sleep march. Repeating his name over and over, he followed the owls in his group and now moved into the shadow of the overhang of the arch. "Ah," Soren sighed. The stabbing feeling in his skull ceased. His gizzard grew still. And Soren became more alert, the proper state for an owl who lived in the night. He looked about him. The little Spotted Owl named Hortense stood next to him. "Hortense?" Soren said. She stared at him blankly and began tapping her feet as if to move.

A sleep monitor swooped down. "Whatcha marching in place for, 12-8? Assume the sleeping position."

Hortense immediately tipped her beak up, her head slightly back, but there was no moon to shine down upon it in the shadow of the rock. Soren, also in the sleep position, slid his eyes toward her. *Curious*, he thought. She responded to her number name but not her old name, except to move her feet. Still unable to sleep in this newfangled position, Soren twisted his head about to survey the stone arch. Through the other side of the arch, he caught sight of Gylfie, but too late. The alarm sounded, a high, piercing shriek. Before he knew it, he was being pushed along as thousands of owls began to move. Within seconds, there was an indescribable babble as each owl repeated its old name over and over again.

It became clear to Soren that they were following the path of the moon around the glaucidium. There were, however, so many owls that they could not all be herded under the full shine of the moon at the same time. Therefore, some were allowed an interval under the overhang of the rock arch. Perhaps he and Gylfie, since they had wound up before at the arch at the same time, could meet there again. He was determined to get close to Gylfie the next time.

But that would take three more times. Three more times of blathering his name into the moonlit night. Three more times of feeling the terrible twinge in his gizzard. "12-1, tip that beak up!" It was a sleep monitor. He felt a thwack to the side of his head. Hortense was still next to him. She mumbled, "12-8, what a lovely name that is. 12-8, perfect name. I love twos and fours and eights. So smooth."

"Hortense," Soren whispered softly. Her talons might have just vaguely begun to stir on the floor, but other than that, nothing. "Hort! Horty!" He tried, but the little Spotted Owl was lost in some dreamless sleep.

Finally, Soren was back under the arch and quickly moved over to the other side, which connected to the neighboring glaucidium. The sleep monitors had just barked out the command, "Now, sleep!"

Suddenly, Gylfie was there. The tiny Elf Owl swung her head toward Soren. "They're moon blinking us," she whispered.

CHAPTER FIVE

Moon Blinking

W hat?" It felt so good to say a *whh* sound that Soren almost missed the answer.

"Didn't your parents tell you about the dangers of sleeping under the full shine?"

"What is 'full shine'?" Soren asked.

"When did you hatch out?"

"Three weeks ago, I think. Or so my parents told me." But again, Soren was not really sure what a week was.

"Ah, that explains it. And in Tyto there are great trees, right?" Gylfie asked.

"Oh, yes. Many, and thick with beautiful fir needles and spruce cones and leaves that turn golden and red." Again, Soren wasn't sure about leaves turning for he had never seen them anything but golden and red. But his parents had told him that once they were green in a time called summer. Kludd had hatched out near the end of the green time.

"Well, you see, I hatched out more than three weeks

ago." They spoke softly, so softly, and managed to maintain the sleep position, but neither one of them was the least bit sleepy. "I was hatched after the time of newing."

"The newing? When is that?" asked Soren.

"You see, the moon comes and the moon goes, and at the time of the newing, when the moon is no thicker than one single thin, downy feather, well, that is the first glint of the new moon. Then, every day it grows thicker and fatter until there is full shine, like now. And it might stay that way for three or four days. Then comes the time of the dwenking. Instead of growing thicker and fatter, the moon dwenks and becomes thinner, until, once more, it is no thicker than the thinnest strand of down. And then it disappears for a while."

"I never saw this. At least, I don't think I have."

"Oh, it was there but you probably didn't *really* see because your family's nest was in the hollow of a great tree in a thick forest. But Elf Owls like myself live in deserts. Not so many trees. And many of them are not very leafy. We can see the whole sky nearly all the time."

"My!" Soren sighed softly.

"And that is why they teach all of us Elf Owls about full shine. Although most owls sleep during the day, sometimes, especially after a hunting expedition, one might be tired and sleep at night. This can be very dangerous if one sleeps out bald in the light of a full moon. It confuses one's head."

"How?" Soren asked.

"I'm not sure. My parents never really explained it but they did say that the old owl Rocmore had gone crazy from too much full shine." Gylfie paused, then hesitating, went on. "They even said that he often did not know which was up and which was down and that finally he died of a broken neck when he thought he was lifting off from the top of a cactus." Gylfie's voice almost broke here. "He thought he was flying toward the stars and he slammed into the earth. That's what moon blinking is all about. You no longer know what is for sure and what is not. What is truth and what are lies. What is real and what is false. That is being moon blinked."

Soren gasped. "This is awful! Is this what is going to happen to us?"

"Not if we can help it, Soren."

"What can we do?"

"I'm not sure. Let me think a while. Meanwhile, try to cock your head just a bit, so the moon does not shine straight down on it. And remember, when flying in full shine there is no problem. But sleeping in it is disastrous."

"I can't fly yet," Soren said softly.

"Well, just be sure you don't sleep."

Soren cocked his head and while doing so tipped his beak down to look upon the little Elf Owl. *How,* he wondered, *was such a tiny creature so smart?* He hoped with all his might that Gylfie would come up with something. Some idea. Just as he was thinking this, there was a sharp bark. "12-1, head straight, beak up!" It was another sleep monitor. He felt a thwack to the side of his head. They did not fall asleep, and as soon as the patrolling owl left, they began whispering again. But then, all too soon, came the inevitable alarm for a sleep march to begin. It would be three more circuits before they could meet again under the arch.

"Remember what I told you. Don't sleep."

"I'm so tired. How can I help it?"

"Think of anything."

"What?"

"Anything —" Gylfie hesitated before a sleep monitor shoved her along. "Think of flying!"

Flying, yes, thinking of flying would keep Soren awake. There was nothing more exciting. But in the meantime, all thoughts of flight were drowned out by the sound of his own voice repeating his own name.

"Soren . . . Soren . . . Soren. . . . Soren . . ." There was also the sound of thousands of talons clicking on the hard stone surface as they marched in lines. Soren was between

Hortense and a Horned Owl whose name blended into the drone of other names. Three Snowy Owls were directly in front of him. There were perhaps twenty or more owls to each group, all arranged in loose lines, but they moved in unison as one block of owls, each owl endlessly repeating his or her name. It was impossible to sort out an individual name from the babble, and it was not long when, on the fourth sleep march, his own name began to sound odd to Soren. Within another one hundred or so times of repeating it, it seemed almost as if it was not a name at all. It was merely a noise. And he, too, was becoming a meaningless creature with no real name, no family, but ... but ... but maybe a friend?

Finally, they stopped again. And it was in the silence of that moment when they stopped that Soren suddenly realized what was happening. It all made sense, particularly when he thought of what Gylfie had explained to him about moon blinking. This alone would keep him awake until he met up with her again.

"They are moon blinking us with our names, Gylfie," Soren gasped as he edged in close to the little owl under the stone arch. Only the stars twinkled above. Gylfie understood immediately. A name endlessly repeated became a meaningless sound. It completely lost its individuality, its significance. It would dissolve into nothingness. Soren continued, "Just move your beak or say your number, but don't say your name. That way it will stay your name." There would, however, be at least three more nights of full shine and then the fullness would begin to lessen until the moon was completely dwenked.

Gylfie looked at Soren in amazement. This ordinary Barn Owl was in his own way quite extraordinary. This was absolutely brilliant. Gylfie felt more than ever compelled to figure out a solution to sleeping exposed to full shine.

CHAPTER SIX

Separate Pits, One Mind

When Soren and Gylfie parted at the end of that long night, they looked at each other and blinked, trembling with fear. If only they could be together in the same pit, then they could think together, talk, and plan. Gylfie had told Soren a little about her pit. She, too, had a pit guardian who seemed very nice, at least compared to Jatt and Jutt or Skench. Gylfie's pit guardian was called Unk, short for Uncle and, like Auntie, he tried to arrange special treats for Gylfie — a bit of snake sometimes, often even calling Gylfie by her real name and not her number, 25-2. Indeed, when Gylfie had told Soren how her pit guardian had asked her to call him "Unk" it was almost identical to the way in which Aunt Finny had insisted on Soren calling her "Auntie."

"It was all so weird," Gylfie had said. "I called him sir at first, and then he said, 'Sir! All this formality. Really, now! Remember what I asked you to call me? 'Uncle,' I answered. 'Now . . . now . . . I gave you my special name.'"

The special name was Unk and the way in which Gylfie described Unk drawing that name of endearment from her, well, Soren could just imagine the Great Horned Owl dipping low to be on eye level with the little Elf Owl, the huge tufts above his ears nearly scraping the ground.

"The pit guardians go out of their way to be nice to us," Soren had said. "But it's still kind of scary, isn't it?"

"Very!" Gylfie had replied. "It was after I called him Unk that he gave me the bits of snake." She had then sighed. "I remember so well, as if it was yesterday, my First Snake ceremony. Dad had saved the rattles for me and my sisters to play with. And you know what, Soren? It was as if Unk had read my mind because I was thinking about my ceremony and just then he says, 'I might even have some rattles for you to play with.' And then I thanked him. I over-thanked him. It was disgusting, Soren."

And Soren knew just what the little Elf Owl meant.

But now they were separated and Soren hoped desperately that Gylfie would come up with some solution. And Gylfie, once more stuffed with some extra snake bits that Unk had given her, had become very drowsy in her pit. Unk had even allowed her to sneak in some extra sleep — another little treat, or was it a bribe? But Gylfie could not sleep. She would be on the brink of sleep, drowsy with the succulent snake meat she had gorged on — much too much for an owl of her size, but just as she was about to fall asleep something would prick her dim consciousness, some thought. Soren, in the pit next door, was concentrating as hard as he could. *"Think of something, Gylfie! Think of something!"*

Auntie had been so nice. When Soren returned to the stone pit, she had said that she'd never seen a more tired-looking owl. "Didn't sleep a wink, huh?"

"'Fraid not, Auntie," Soren had replied.

"Now, you hear me. Why don't you hop up there in that little stone niche, just your size and out of prying eyes, and take yourself a little blink or two?"

"You mean sleep?" The question just slipped out. "Sorry about the question."

"Of course, dear, I mean sleep and don't apologize about the question. We'll get stricter with that later."

"But it's against the rules. We're suppose to be getting ready for our work assignments."

"Sometimes rules are made to be broken. In my opinion, they should go much easier on you owlets after you first arrive. You're orphans, for Glaux's sake."

It still disturbed Soren deeply to be called an orphan.

He had a mother and a father and a sister and a brother. He wasn't sure why, but there was something shameful about being called an orphan, especially when one wasn't. It was as if you were this disconnected, unloved creature.

"I know," Auntie continued. "I'm just an old broody." *What was a broody?* Soren wondered, but he suppressed the urge to ask. Soren hopped up into the stone niche. *My goodness,* he thought. *I did that rather well. Could have passed my branching test on that one.* And then he became very sad when he thought that he had not even been able to begin his first branching lessons with his father.

Sleep indeed was hard to come by — even a blink or two, because when Soren started to think about branching, he, of course, could not help but think about flying and remembered watching Kludd's attempts and finally his first very small flight. Something pushed at the back of Soren's brain, a memory. Soren was not sure how long he had been sleeping but it was not Auntie who woke him up. It was something else, something unspeakable. Once more he felt that terrible queasiness mixed with dread. It was as if his gizzard might burst. But the terrible truth settled like a stone inside him. Kludd had pushed him! It came to him in a flash. So real that he could still feel the swift kick of Kludd's talons in his side and then pitching over the edge of the hollow.

His legs began to shake. Auntie was at his side. "Need to yarp, dear?"

"Yes," Soren said weakly. He yarped a miserable little pellet. What did he expect? He had never even had his First Bones ceremony, which again made him remember all of Kludd's strutting about when he yarped his first pellet with bones. Would they have such things as First Bones ceremonies here? They did everything so strangely. The Number ceremony, for example. They called that a ceremony! Ceremonies were supposed to make you feel special. The Number ceremony hadn't made him feel anything. Auntie Finny was nice, but the others really weren't so nice at all, and this orphanage business — what was that all about? What was the real purpose of St. Aggie's? Skench, the Ablah General, said, "When Truth Is Found, Purpose Is Revealed." No questions, just be humble. The only truth that Soren knew right now was a deep gizzard-chilling one: His brother had shoved him from the nest. *Think, Gylfie,* thought Soren. *Think of something!*

CHAPTER SEVEN
The Great Scheme

Pretend to march, Soren. That is what we must do!"

It was just after the first rising shriek had been sounded by the brutish Great Horned Owl, who perched on one of the outcroppings. Soren and Gylfie had met at the stone ledge for morning food rations.

"What do you mean, pretend to march?" Soren blinked. Between the horrible truth about his brother and missing his parents, Soren could hardly hear what Gylife was saying. His head was filled with the thoughts of his parents. It seemed as if every hour he found a new, more painful way to miss them. *One*, he decided, *did not get used to missing parents*. The thought of never seeing his mum or da again was the most unbearable thing he knew. And yet he could not stop thinking of them. He did not want to stop thinking of them. He would never stop thinking of them.

"Listen to me, Soren. It came to me first that the reason for the march is because of the shadows cast from the high cliffs into the glaucidium, and the arch is always in the shadows. Right?"

"Right." Soren nodded.

"We are forced to march so that no one group of owls will spend too much time under these shadowy shields against the moon's light. I remembered what you said, how we must pretend to say our names but instead we actually repeat our numbers. And then it was easy. We have to pretend to march but never move, so we stay under the protection of the shadows. I suddenly remembered how my father, who was a great navigator, one of the best in the entire Desert of Kuneer, had tried to explain to me that stars and even the moon do not move in the way they seem to from our view on Earth. Some stars, my father said, even appear to stand still in the sky, but, in fact, they do move."

"Huh?" Soren grunted.

"Look, I know it's a little weird, but my da explained that this was because of the great distance that disguises in stillness a star's motion. Even the moon, my father said, which is closer than many stars, is so distant that we cannot see the wobbles in its path as it glides through the night. So, don't you see that if the motion of something as big as the moon could be disguised, well, couldn't the motion of something as small as us be disguised?"

A new light began to glimmer in Soren's eyes. Gylfie grew more excited. "We can be like the stars, only in reverse. In other words, what would happen if we just stayed still and pretended to march — if we marched in place?"

"What about the monitors?" Soren asked.

"I've thought about that. The monitors always stand at the edges of the mass of marching owls. They don't really see what is going on in the middle. I saw a Grass Owl stumble last night. No one said, 'Oh, sorry' or 'Move it!' or 'You clumsy bird.' All the owls simply parted and went around the Grass Owl. So what if we pretend to march and stay under the shadow of the arch each time? Get it? We would march in place and give the appearance of motion."

"It's a great scheme, Gylfie!" Soren's voice was filled with awe.

"We'll try it tonight. I can't wait," Gylfie said. "But I'm hungry now."

"This is it?" Soren blinked as a large rusty-colored owl shoved one dead cricket toward him on the stone ledge. "I mean, this is it!" Soren quickly said, correcting what had been a question, as he stared down at what St. Aggie's called breakfast. No mouse meat, no fat worms — oh, for a hummingbird! But one cricket! This was ridiculous. He would starve.

As the owlets stopped to eat, there was only the sound of their beaks crunching the crickets. Soren couldn't believe that no one talked. Owlets always talked when they ate. His little sister, Eglantine, jabbered so much sometimes that his mum had to remind her to eat. "Eat the feet on that bug, Eglantine. Eat the feet. You talk so much you're missing the very best part of the beetle."

So the silence began to bother him and there was indeed a terrible quiet to the stone canyons that made up St. Aggie's. Always, of course, there was the hollow whistle of the wind and the endless clicking of talons on the hard rock surfaces. Other than that, there was not much sound. Instead, there was an overwhelming sense of being cut off, separated from Earth, and even from sky. Soren began to realize that the entire lives of these owls, if one could call it living, were carried out in the deep stone boxes and slots, the canyons and ravines of St. Aggie's. There was very little water — just a trickle here and there into which they could dip their beaks for a drink. There were no leaves, no mosses that he could see, no grasses — none of the soft things that wrapped the world and made it tender and springy. It was a stone forest with its jagged outcroppings, rock needles, and spires and ledges.

They had almost finished eating, so there was not even the clicking, just the sound of crickets being crunched.

An owl next to him muttered, "I'd love a little piece of rat snake."

"Oooh." Soren sighed and thought of Mrs. Plithiver. His family avoided serving snake out of respect for Mrs. Plithiver. Mrs. Plithiver said it was nonsense. "Show me a rat snake or a bull snake that anyone really loved." She would say, "Don't worry about my feelings. I have no feeling toward such snakes." But still his parents avoided such foods. Soren's father called it "species sensitivity." Soren had no idea what that meant, except he didn't want to hurt Mrs. Plithiver's feelings and she had just said she had none. Soren, of course, didn't really believe this. He thought Mrs. Plithiver had plenty of feelings. She was a most lovable creature, and his heart beat a little harder when he remembered her calling down to him from the hollow high in the fir tree. It almost made him cry to remember her voice. What had happened to her that night? Had Kludd done something to her as well? Or had she gotten away to get help? Did she miss him? Did his parents miss him? Once more, there was that sharp pain of missing and Soren nearly staggered with the very idea of never seeing his parents. Then he thought of Kludd and began to tremble all over again.

"You all right?" Gylfie asked. She was so small that she barely reached up to Soren's wing tips.

"No, I'm not all right," Soren gasped. "Nothing is right. Don't you miss your parents? Don't you wonder what they think happened to you?"

"Yes, yes. I just can't think about it," Gylfie replied. "Listen, pull yourself together. We have our Great Scheme, remember?"

"What do you mean pull yourself together? Do you know what I just figured out about my brother?"

"Look, we don't have much time," Gylfie said quickly. "Make sure you get assigned to the pelletorium."

"The pelletorium?" Soren said blankly.

CHAPTER EIGHT
The Pelletorium

Auntie Finny suddenly appeared. "Cricket hunter. You're perfect. You see, here in our lovely stone country the cricket season is much longer. They hide in the nooks and crannies and then come out in the sunshine to bask in the heat of the day."

"Uh . . ." Soren started to speak. "I'm feeling a little peckish, you know, Auntie. I think maybe the pelletorium would be better for me."

"Oh, the pelletorium!" Auntie Finny looked slightly confused. She had never had an owlet suggest another workstation or training schedule. She looked at the Barn Owl. He didn't look well. And if he failed as a cricket hunter, it would reflect poorly on her. And then again, if she fulfilled this owl's request, it would perhaps put him in her debt. It was always good to have an owlet indebted to you. "Yes, yes. I suppose so." She gazed at the young owl. Soren felt the soft yellow glow of her eyes. "Now, remember, dear, what I've done for you and remember the little" —

61

she beaked the word — "'nap' I allowed you." The yellow light turned a bit hard like glinting gold. "Then follow that line over there into the pelletorium."

"I am 47-2. I am to be your guide for the pelletorium. Follow me." The owlet spoke in a peculiar manner. Her sounds were clipped and hollow. It was not like the terrible thrum and clang of Jatt and Jutt, but it was like no owl sound Soren had ever heard.

Soren and Gylfie followed number 47-2, who had begun to march. Soon, they heard the *click* of all the owlets' talons as they struck the ground, for they were once more marching in time. Now the strange hollow tone in which 47-2 had spoken seemed to hover over the vast marching assembly of owlets. They were singing!

Every pellet has a story all its own.
Every pellet has a story all its own.
With its fur and teeth and bones
And one or two stones,
Every pellet has a story all its own.

We shall dissect every pellet with glee.
Perhaps we'll find a rodent's knee.
And never shall we tire

In the sacred task that we conspire,
Nor do our work less than perfectly
And those bright flecks at the core,
Which make our hearts soar,
Shall forever remain the deepest mystery.

Nothing could have prepared Soren and Gylfie for the shock of what met their eyes as they entered the pelletorium. They had been led into another box canyon, and on slabs of rock ledges hundreds of owls bobbed their heads up and down over thousands of pellets that had been yarped by owls. If either one of these two little owlets had known the meaning of the word "hell," they would have known that this was certainly the deepest and worst part of it. But neither Soren nor Gylfie in their short lives knew of such things as hell or the words that would describe such a place. Until their snatching, they really had only known what might be called heaven. Life high in a lovely tree hollow or cactus lined with the downy fluff of their parents, plump insects delivered several times a day, and then the first juicy mouse morsels. And besides all the delicious meals, there were stories — stories of flight, of learning to fly, of the feeling that must be deep in their gizzards in order to rise on the wind.

Number 47-2 stepped up to them and, in her weirdly

hollow voice, she began to speak. "I am what is called a third-degree picker. I pick through the pellets for the larger objects — pebbles, bone, and teeth mostly. Second-degree pickers pick for feathers and fur. First-degree pickers pick for flecks. This is a fleck." 47-2 pointed with her talon to the tiniest speck that glinted in an open pellet. "It is a kind of metal." She paused. "Or something," she added vaguely. "You need not know what they are. You need only know that flecks are precious, more precious than gold. To become a fleck picker is the highest level of skill in the pelletorium. Tomorrow I shall be advanced one level. I shall be a second-degree picker. Therefore, as the most advanced third-degree picker, it is my task to instruct you." And then the owlet blinked. She began humming the dreadful song.

"It is best when beginning as a picker to use your beak. Your talons can be used to steady the pellet. Each object you find is to be lined up neatly on the stone ledge — your work area. Failure to line up objects neatly is a most serious offense. Offenders are severely punished, as shall be demonstrated during our laughter therapy sessions."

Soren and Gylfie had no idea what this owlet was talking about. Laughter therapy? "Do your work diligently and you, too, may be advanced someday." The owlet then stepped up to the ledge, which was covered with pellets, and bent over one. "Proceed. It is strictly forbidden to use your own pellets in this work." 47-2 glared at Soren. The owlet bent her speckled head and began to pick.

Soren felt a gagging sensation and yarped another pellet.

Soren and Gylfie had no idea how long they had been working. It seemed endless. It was not entirely quiet, however. At certain intervals, a low soft whistle alarm would be sounded from one of the smaller owls who monitored the work from overhead ledges and the sound of another pellet song would begin to rise. The songs were sung in the same hollow tones in which 47-2 had spoken. But Soren felt that they were sung mostly to provide a rhythm for their work. The words, he supposed, like their own non-number names, had become meaningless. In between the songs it was not completely silent. There were, of course, certain commands that had to be given. "New pellets needed in area 10-B." Or "Area 20-C needs to pick up the pace." And then there was some talk among the owls as they worked, but the more carefully Soren and Gylfie listened, the stranger this talk seemed. And then suddenly an owlet working at the same ledge as Soren began to speak. "12-1. I feel perfect this morning. I have just completed my first set of pellets. I am sure you shall feel perfect, too, when you have completed your first set. It is a feeling of rare contentment to complete a set. I feel this sense of rare contentment every morning at this hour."

Rare? Soren thought. That was a word he knew, for his parents had told them that the family of Barn Owls to which they belonged, the Tyto Alba, had become rare, which meant there were not many of them. So how could this owlet's contentment be rare if it happened every morning at a particular hour?

"I, too, feel perfect." Another owlet now spoke, turning toward Gylfie this time. It was nearly the same speech.

At regular intervals now, the two owls turned alternately to Soren and Gylfie and gave short little reports on their states of contentment. On occasion, these reports became interspersed with comments. "25-2, for an owlet of your exceedingly tiny stature you have a fine posture as you peck."

"Thank you," Gylfie replied, and dipped her head in what she thought was a docile manner.

"You are most welcome, 25-2."

Then the owlet closest to Soren began, "12-1, your beak work is quite advanced. You work with industry and delicacy."

"Thank you," said Soren. And then for some reason he added, "Thank you very much."

"You're welcome. But you need not be excessively polite. It wastes energy. Politeness is its own reward — just like flecks."

"What are flecks?" The question slipped out, but many of the pellet songs referred to flecks and Soren could not understand for the life of him what they were. He understood the feathers and bones and teeth being found in the pellets, but what were these mysterious flecks? The two owlets each gave small piercing shrieks that contrasted sharply with their usual tones. "Question alarm! Question alarm!" Two ferocious, darkly feathered owls, their glaring yellow eyes framed above by dark red eye tufts, swooped down and plucked up Soren.

"How could you, Soren?" Gylfie nearly cried out, but luckily the question died on her beak.

Soren felt as if his gizzard were dropping to his talons as the two owls soared with him dangling between them. They were transporting him in a most painful manner. Each one held a wing in his talons and it was as if he were being torn in half! And as they spiraled upward in the pelletorium, Soren felt beneath him not the cushion of captured air of which his father had often spoken, but instead a surge of noisy vibrations that seem to pummel him from below.

"They are laughing at you, 12-1. They laugh so hard the air is tossed with their chuckles!" said one of the owls.

"You, 12-1," the other owl was speaking now. "You are our first object of the day for laughter therapy." Soren remained mute. No matter how many questions might batter his brain, his imagination, or dance on the tip of his beak, he would never ask them. The two owls had now alighted with him on a very high ledge that was visible to the entire pelletorium below. The laughter of the owlets and the scores of monitors and guards ricocheted off the stone walls. It filled Soren's head with a terrible clatter. He thought he would go yoicks right there and start screaming.

"And now for the best moment of all in laughter therapy!" There was a shrill screech. The air stirred, and Skench, the Ablah General, landed next to Soren. And then Skench's second-in-command, Lieutenant Spoorn, arrived, eyes darting in an amber glee. *Oh, great Glaux!* thought Soren. *What now?*

CHAPTER NINE
Good Nurse Finny

O h, 12-1! Oh, my goodness! Look at you." Soren groaned and blinked.

"What happened?" Soren asked. His eyes fluttered open and he felt himself basking in the tender yellow light of Auntie Finny's eyes.

"Now, now, dear. Questions are what got you into trouble in the first place. We'll have to be a little stricter. All you need to know is that you were naughty and now you're back with me in the stone pit and ..." A soft babble of soothing hoots streamed from Auntie's beak. But one question after the next pounded inside Soren's head. He nearly had to clamp his beak shut not to ask them. He must have fainted at some point during the laughter therapy session. He was trying to reconstruct what had happened in his head. There had been the question alarm, the two ferocious beaks, the laughter — oh, the laughter had been terrible — but why were his wings hurting so much? This time the question simply withered in his mind, not because he was too frightened to ask but because he had turned his head and seen his wings. Bare! "Great Glaux!" he muttered, and promptly fell over once more in a faint.

"Now, now!" Auntie Finny was clicking her beak. "I'm going to take care of that. You'll feel better in no time. You don't need those silly little feathers."

"Don't need my feathers!" It was not a question. Was this owl totally yoicks? "Don't need my feathers," he repeated, and was about to ask how he would ever fly, but he clamped his beak shut tight. Auntie was now crushing something in her beak. She gave a yarp-like hiccup and a pulpy wad of soggy moss flew from her beak directly onto Soren's wings. It felt good and Soren sighed. "Nice feeling, yes it is. Nothing like this stone moss for curing what ails you. Now you can call me Nursey."

"Nursey?" And then Soren corrected himself. "Oh, Nursey!"

"You're learning, dear. You're learning fast. Sometimes we do have to be a little stricter. But I bet you've learned your lesson and you'll never get plucked again."

"Plucked!" Soren gasped. They had actually plucked him? This wasn't an accident?

"I know! I know what you're thinking. I really don't approve. But you know I have very little say. I can only do my best for each and every little owlet in my pit. I try. I try." She almost whimpered.

But Auntie or Nursey didn't know what Soren was thinking, not at all. She looked at him kindly. She asked no questions, of course, but Soren felt compelled to say, "Auntie . . . I mean, Nursey." Names seemed awfully important to this old Snowy Owl. Very carefully, he was going to try to explain his thoughts without asking questions — oh, he had indeed learned his lesson. "I do not understand, Nursey, why you are so nice here in the stone pit and they are so awful, the owls in the glaucidium and the pelletorium. They are mean for no good reason."

"Ah, but there is a reason."

"There is a reason." Soren's words were flat and carried no inflection of a question. This was indeed possible.

"You see," Nursey Finny continued, "it builds character."

"It builds character," Soren repeated in the same even tone.

"Through carefully meted-out punishment and self-denial, you shall be made hardy." Nursey spoke in a singsong voice as if she had said these same words many times before.

"Destroying wings builds character. I see." Soren tried to sound logical and keep any hint of the incredulous out of his voice.

"Oh, yes, you do see. I am so pleased."

"And to think I always thought flight was a natural part of an owl's character. Silly me." He was getting awfully good at this.

"Oh, you are a bright little thing," Nursey hooted cheerfully. "You're catching on. Yes, flight is to be earned if one is destined for flight at all."

"Yes, yes, of course," Soren said, trying desperately to keep the reasonable tone in his voice. But inside, his gizzard was twitching madly, his heart was beating rapidly, and a dark panic began to fill him.

"Oh, and here comes 12-8. A fine example of a DNF."

Soren stared at her with incomprehension.

"DNF, dear. It means Destined Not to Fly. 12-8 is one. And a nursey in training, too!"

Who was number 12-8? Soren sorted through all the numbers in his mind. The number sounded familiar and then Soren saw the little Spotted Owl named Hortense, who was so happy to receive her number designation because she hated her name. She was hopping about nearby.

"Come here, 12-8. Your first nursing lesson," Auntie trilled.

Hortense, or number 12-8, had an even blanker look than ever in her eyes. "Ooh, a patient! A patient! Show me how to make moss pulp."

Finny began to show the little owl how to beak the moss until it was soft and squishy. Soren had to admit he didn't mind the attention to his wings that indeed were feeling much better. He observed 12-8 carefully as she applied the moss compresses. He wondered why she was not destined for flight. He carefully tried to figure out how to get the answer without asking a question. "I saw you, I think, in the pelletorium this morning."

"Oh, no, no, not me! I'm strictly a broody."

"A broody," Soren repeated. Only silence followed. "A broody," Soren repeated again. Still silence. "It must be nice to be a broody, to work in the *broodorium*." Soren just made up the word.

"It's not called a broodorium." 12-8 spoke in the perfect hollow tones of the truly moon blinked.

"Oh, it isn't," Soren said flatly. "Yes, how stupid of me. It's that other word. Slips my mind right now."

"No, it doesn't slip your mind. You don't know. No one does." 12-8's voice had turned brittle. "Top secret."

"Top secret."

"Top secret. I've got clearance." The little owl swelled up now with pride.

"Flight clearance."

"Absolutely not! That is stupid. I couldn't have top secret clearance if I had flight clearance." *But don't you want to fly?* Soren was ready to scream the question. Just then, Finny returned.

"Ah, 12-8, you are doing a splendid job. What a little nurse you'll make."

"My wings do feel a lot better," Soren said sweetly, and marveled how deceptive he was quickly becoming. Oh, yes, his wings did feel better, but Soren had another idea, another question he wanted to throw out under the guise of a statement. "I'll tell you the thing that really always perks me up and makes me feel just fine in the gizzard."

"Oh, that's what we want, my dear," Finny cooed.

"A story. My favorite stories are the legends of Ga'Hoole. Yes, the Ga'Hoolian cycle, I think they are called."

A strange sound halfway between a yarp and the screech of a Screech Owl issued from Auntie Finny's beak, and she crumpled into a dead faint.

"Oh, my goodness! Oh, my goodness. I don't know what you said, 12-1, but I've got to nurse Nursey now." The little Spotted Owl trotted off to find a remedy.

"I know what I said," Soren whispered to himself. "I said, 'the legends of Ga'Hoole.'"

CHAPTER TEN

Right Side Up in an Upside-down World

The next night, Gylfie and Soren met under the arch of the glaucidium. They were to begin the Great Scheme, but Soren suddenly had doubts.

"I'm really worried, Gylfie. It might not work."

"Soren," Gylfie pleaded, "who knows if it will work or not, but what have we got to lose if we don't try it?"

"Our minds, to start with," Soren replied. Gylfie gave the soft *churrr* sound of a chuckle that is nearly universal for all owls.

There was a swoosh in the air and suddenly the little Elf Owl was flat on her back. "There is no laughing. Laughter may only be practiced under the direction of Lieutenant Spoorn. Don't do it again. Next time you shall be reported immediately, and I shall anticipate eagerly your first lesson in correct laughter."

The monitor then moved away. Soren and Gylfie

looked at each other wordlessly. This had to be the strangest place imaginable. They taught one how to sleep! Lessons in laughter! Laughter therapy! Soren wondered what possibly could be the purpose of a place like St. Aggie's. What were they really learning to do here and why? What were the flecks, more precious than gold? What were Skench and Spoorn trying to turn them into? Not owls, for sure! But there was not time to dwell on that. Soren had another matter that had been bothering him more and more since his own laughter therapy session.

"Gylfie, you can get out, maybe, but not me. But you can."

"What are you talking about, Soren?"

"Gylfie, you are just a short time from being fully fledged — look at you. I think you've budged some more beginning primaries today. You'll be able to leave soon."

"And so will you."

"What are you talking about? I think you have been moon blinked. They just plucked my feathers, Gylfie."

"They plucked your down. Look, your primary shaft points are still there, and I see some secondary ones, too."

Soren lifted one wing and examined it. There were still budging points. Gylfie was right on this. *But*, Soren wondered, *without down what...?*

It was as if Gylfie had read his thoughts. "You don't

need down to fly, Soren. Down just keeps you warm. You can fly without it. It'll just be cold, and who knows? By the time your flight feathers really come in, you'll probably have some more down."

Soren blinked again. For the first time, there was hope in the dark eyes set like polished stones in his white heart-shaped face, and something quickened in Gylfie's own heart. She had to convince Soren that he could do this. She had to make him really believe in the Great Scheme.

Gylfie had watched as her older brothers and sisters had reached that point, when they seemed to mysteri-ously gather strength and lift into flight after days of end-less hopping. She remembered asking her father how they did it. Now her father's words came back to her:

"Gylf, you can practice forever and still never fly if you do not really believe you can. That is what gives you that feeling in the gizzard." Then her father had stopped and, in a musing tone of voice, said, "Funny isn't it, how all our strongest feelings come through our gizzards — even a feeling that is about our wings." He had ruffled a few of his flight feathers as if to demonstrate. "It all comes through our gizzard," he had repeated.

"Listen to me, Soren," Gylfie said. "I found out a lot in the pelletorium after you fainted and they had to carry you out."

Soren blinked and shivered his shoulders in the way young owls do when they are embarrassed or ashamed. "Yes, Gylfie, while I was stupidly asking questions you were listening."

"Quit beating up on yourself," Gylfie said sharply. "They've already done that." Gylfie's directness shocked Soren. He stopped blinking and looked straight at the Elf Owl. "Look. What did I just tell you? Everything here at St. Aggie's is upside down and inside out. It's our job not to get moon blinked and to stand right side up in an upside-down world. If we don't do that we'll never be able to escape. We'll never be able to think. And thinking is the only way we'll be able to plan an escape. So listen to me." Soren nodded and Gylfie continued. "Now first, I have figured out that tonight is the third night of full shine. In fact, the moon has already started to dwenk. Remember, I told you about this. You'll see that in a few days it shall almost disappear and we won't have to worry about being moon blinked. Every night in the glaucidium, it will become darker and darker and easier and easier for us to find the shadows. But in the meantime, we must act as if we are moon blinked."

Soren resisted asking a question even though he knew there was no danger with Gylfie. But still, he simply did not want to break into Gylfie's thoughts. It was clear to

Soren that this Elf Owl might be very small in every way but her ideas. And he could tell that Gylfie was thinking very hard now.

"After one more newing," Gylfie continued, "you shall be very close to having fledged all of your flight feathers, and certainly by the time of full shine, you shall be ready to fly."

"But what about you, Gylfie? You will be ready in a few days."

"I shall wait for you."

"Wait for me!" It was not a question. Soren was simply shocked. Too shocked to even speak. So finally it was Gylfie who asked the question.

"What's wrong, Soren?"

"Gylfie, I cannot believe what you just said. Why would you wait for me when you can get out of here?"

"That's just the point, Soren. I would never leave you behind. You are my friend, first of all. If I escaped without you, my life would not be worth two pellets to me. And second, we need each other."

"I need you more than you need me," Soren said in a small voice.

"Oh, racdrops!" Once more Soren could hardly believe his ears. Racdrops, short for raccoon droppings, was one of the most daring, dirtiest, worst words an owlet could say. Kludd had gotten thumped good and hard by his mother when Mrs. Plithiver had reported that he had said "racdrops" to her when she insisted he stop teasing Eglantine.

"Soren, you were the one who realized that they were trying to moon blink us with our own names by having us repeat them. That was brilliant."

"But you were the one who knew about moon blinking in the first place. I'd never heard of it."

"I just knew something that you didn't. That's not thinking, just happening to know it. You would have known it if you had been hatched a little earlier or lived in the desert. But now I learned something new. You see, Soren," Gylfie continued, "after they took you away, I made a discovery. That owlet 47-2, she sent me on an errand. It was outside the pelletorium and . . ." Gylfie looked about, then continued her tale in a low voice. The first shine of the moon was just beginning to slither over the dark horizon.

CHAPTER ELEVEN

Gylfie's Discovery

I was supposed to go and tell the pellet gatherers that new trays were needed in our area. So 47-2 pointed me in the direction of what she called the Big Crack. It was, in fact, very near our area and ran straight up a rock side of the pelletorium. I was told to go into the crack and I would find a line of other owlets also going to the storerooms and to follow them and not go off the trail. So I did just that."

Gylfie was telling the story so well that Soren could imagine every little turn on the path through the rock crack. It was as if he were right there with Gylfie. . . .

"There were many cracks leading off the main crack and sometimes voices could be heard. It was interesting that none of the other owlets who I followed seemed to even notice these cracks or hear the voices. Perhaps they had walked this trail so often it was meaningless to them. But I looked about and could see that at one point in the crack the sky cut through. Yes, it was quite beautiful, really, just a little piece of sky like a blue river flowing above, and then at one point the sky seemed very low. You know" — Gylfie stopped and mused for a moment — "ever since we have been here, Soren, I have had the feeling that St. Aegolius Academy is deep, deep in a stone canyon. That its very steepness and depth make it the perfect prison. But at this one point along the trail, I realized we were up higher and not so deep. Close to the sky."

"Close to the sky," Soren repeated softly. Once he, too, had been close to the sky. Once he had lived in a hollow high up in a fir tree lined with the fluffy down from his parent's breasts. Once he had lived close to that blueness. That blueness of the day sky and the blackness of the night had been so near. No wonder a little owlet could almost believe it could fly before it really could. The sky was a part of owls and owls were a part of the sky.

Gylfie continued her story. "I thought that on the way back to the pelletorium I would try and look a little harder around this particular spot. Maybe slow down. Then I thought, maybe I could just pretend to be marching. You know, just like the Great Scheme idea. It would be a good test. Would anyone notice? Maybe not and better yet, there did not seem to be any monitors around." Gylfie's eyes brightened and she paused, hoping this idea would sink in with Soren and convince him that it could all work.

"So, on the way back, that is exactly what I did. No one seemed to notice at all. They just moved around me as if I were a part of the stone wall that jutted out. And then something extraordinary happened. An owlet seemed to stumble near me. This owl, a young Snowy, just blinked at me and I thought, 'Great Glaux, I've been discovered standing here.' So I pointed up toward the sky — as if I were admiring the view. "'Sky,' I said pleasantly. And the owl blinked, not a question blink, but a real moon blink. The same look that is in their eyes when they repeat their names on the sleep march." Gylfie took a deep breath, as if what she was about to say was terribly important. And it was. "I realized then that many words for these owlets, just like their names, have no meaning, no meaning at all. Can you imagine, Soren, an owl not knowing what the sky is?"

Soren thought for a moment. It was indeed unimaginable. Or was it? He remembered what Auntie Finny had said about some birds not destined for flight. But Soren had another question. "Does this owlet just not know the word or does she really not know what the sky is?" Gylfie blinked. Soren truly was a deep thinker. He continued, "Mrs. Plithiver, our nest-maid snake, I told you about her, well, she is blind, but she knows about the sky. She says that all snakes, whether they are blind or not, call the sky 'the Yonder' because it is so far away for snakes. It is about as far as anything can be for a snake and that is why she loved working for our family — because she felt close to the Yonder."

"No, Soren, I think this owlet truly has been completely and perfectly moon blinked. She does not know the word, nor does she have any idea of sky."

"That's so sad," Soren said softly.

"It is sad, but you know it makes our job of escaping easier. Maybe the monitors have been moon blinked about words. But I have to tell you the other thing I discovered when I stopped at this place."

"What's that?"

"Well, down a side crack I saw a place that was guarded by an owl who looked familiar. As a matter of fact, I don't know how I didn't recognize him instantly. It was Grimble, the owl who snatched me. I've thought a lot about him. Do you remember what he said when we were flying here, something about it hardly seeming worth the effort and how the owl who snatched you warned him that he might get a demerit if Spoorn heard him talking that way?"

"Yes," Soren said slowly. He was not sure where Gylfie was going with this.

"Well, I think Grimble has perhaps not been perfectly moon blinked and that could be really good, too."

"Wait! One time you say it will be helpful to us if someone is perfectly moon blinked and the next minute you say someone like Grimble, who might not be, can be helpful, too."

"Grimble might be one of us, don't you see, Soren? He might be pretending to be moon blinked the way we have. As a matter of fact, I am almost sure he is."

"Why?"

"Because I went down that side crack and I found out what he was guarding."

"You did?"

"Yes. And do you know how hard it is to find out information when it's against the rules to ask a question?"

"Oh, yes!" Soren said.

"A couple of times I almost did ask questions, and Grimble seemed to sense it."

"What did you find out?"

"Have you ever heard of books?"

"Of course I have," Soren said indignantly. "Books and Barn Owls go very far back." These were the exact words that his parents often said when they took out their few books to read aloud to the owlets. "Especially since so many of us once lived in churches. My parents had a book of psalms."

"Psalms?" Gylfie was truly impressed. "What are psalms?"

"Like songs, sort of, I think." Soren had not really heard that many. But when his mother read him the psalms it seemed that she sang the words more than spoke them. "But what about books? What did you find out from Grimble?"

"The place he guards is a book place. They call it a library. Have you ever heard of that — a library?"

"Never. How did you find out all this? You certainly didn't ask questions."

"No, of course not. You see, it is off-limits. Only Skench and Spoorn are allowed in. That's how I sensed he might be one of us. He seemed to know the question before I ever had to think of a way of asking it. I want to get in."

"Why? I think we just need to get out of here."

"I want to know about the flecks," Gylfie said.

"Flecks? What flecks?"

"The flecks we're always singing about — the bright flecks at the core, the ones the first-degree pickers pick for."

"Are you yoicks, Gylfie? You want to stay around this place long enough to become a first-degree picker?"

"Soren, something worse than just moon blinking

young owls is going on here. I just sense it. Something very bad. Something that could destroy all the kingdoms of all the owls on all the earth." Gylfie paused. "Something deadly." The word seemed to hang in the air, and Gylfie stared ahead unblinkingly.

"These owlets are the walking dead. I think it would be better to be dead than be like 47-2, but you said all the kingdoms of all the owls on all the earth?"

"Total destruction," Gylfie said. Her voice was like ice. "Look, Soren. I want to get out as much as you do. I think Grimble might be helpful, but we'll have to be very careful, and that library with those books holds secrets, secrets I think that could help us escape and maybe help other owls — other owls in your Kingdom of Tyto and mine in the Desert of Kuneer. Would you want any other owls to go through what we've been through?"

Soren suddenly thought of Eglantine. He loved Eglantine. The thought of her being snatched, of being moon blinked, was almost more than he could bear. There was a world of Eglantines out there. Did he really want them to become empty-eyed, hollow-voiced, destined-not-to-fly owls? A shudder ran through Soren. It was not good enough to just escape. In fact, their task was greater than he had ever imagined.

A shriek split the night in the glaucidium. The moon

had risen and the alarm for the first sleep march sounded. Soren and Gylfie felt the stir as thousands of owls began to move. The strange babble rose up as each owl repeated its old name over and over again. The two little owls looked at each other and moved their beaks, turning the sound of their numbers into something that might pass for a name — any name but their own. And now, tonight, they would try the second part of their strategy for the first time. The one that Gylfie had tested in the Big Crack. They would march in place giving the appearance of motion but never moving from the cast shadows. If it had worked for Gylfie in the Big Crack it should work here.

Almost immediately they felt the press of owls about them. They held their breath, fearful that their ruse would be discovered. But the throngs of owls simply parted, just as the waters of a stream split to flow around a rock. They were jostled a bit and they felt a terrible chill as a sleep correction monitor swept by, but the monitor did not look twice at them as they marched in place. No, the monitor seemed only concerned about a small Snowy Owl ahead who had apparently been caught sleeping last time with its head under its wing. "Wing alert on number 85-2. Monitors in the fourth quadrant, please be advised."

CHAPTER TWELVE

Moon Scalding

There was an odd rhythm to the days and the nights at St. Aggies, where owls were expected to sleep at night and work during the day. The moon dwenked, the world darkened, and then once more it was the time of the newing. It was not all dreadful at St. Aggie's. Both Soren and Gylfie were the recipients of extra-special treats, beyond the usual cricket fare, from their pit guardians, Auntie and Unk. Indeed, the time in the pits began to seem like an oasis, verdant and green in the stone world of St. Aegolius Academy for Orphaned Owls. Gylfie received extra rations of snake, the occasional nap was permitted, and Soren, too, was even taught by Auntie how to eat a vole with bones. One could hardly call it a First Bones ceremony. But, nonetheless, Auntie slipped Soren a nice plump vole, just the right length to be swallowed whole. And even though questions were discouraged, Auntie was able to guide Soren through the consuming of his first creature, bones and all. She complimented him lavishly on his first yarped bone pellet. And Soren, of course, was struck by the bittersweet memory of his father complimenting Kludd after his First Bones ceremony.

But despite all the extras, the favors, the gentle coddling from Auntie, Soren could not forget Gylfie's icy voice: "Total destruction. All the kingdoms of all the owls on all the earth." Why? Soren had asked himself often, but then realized it didn't really matter why, if indeed it this was the purpose of St. Aggie's. Even more disturbing was a newer idea of Soren's. *Perhaps*, he thought, *these owls were not really owls at all but rather some kind of demon spirits in a feathered guise.* This was why when Auntie came to him now with his favorite, a plump centipede, Soren stared deep into her yellow eyes as if trying to see the dark antic shadow of a demon. *Are you really an owl, Auntie?* he wanted to ask. *Are you really a true Snowy Owl descended from Glaux, come from the North Kingdoms — or are you a white demon?*

It was the third night of the second full shine now. The full shines seemed to last forever. Soren and Gylfie emerged from these periods of full shines exhausted, but they had somehow managed to resist moon blinking so far. Their strategy for the sleep marches had worked.

Had worked up until this second night of second full shine.

"Right, left. Right, left." They clicked their talons in the precise beat that filled the two glaucidiums as they stood in the overhang of the shared arch.

"Hey, you two!" A hoot shredded the air around them, splitting right through the march. It wasn't Jatt nor was it Jutt. It was none other than Spoorn, Skench's dreadful second-in-command. "I saw you two here last round, and now this round. Lazy, no-good haggards!" Soren and Gylfie, caught in the fierce yellow glare of the Screech Owl's eyes, began to tremble. "Avoiding the moon, that's what I'd say! Well, we have remedies for that."

Oh, Glaux, Soren thought. *If I get plucked again! And Gylfie. She'll never survive it.* "March, you two, march to the moon blaze!"

"Don't say anything," Gylfie whispered. "We're together, that should count for something." *For what?* Soren wondered. *We'll get plucked together? We'll die together?*

The two youngs owls were marched into a stone chamber off to one side of one of the glaucidiums. The walls of this chamber were made of pure white stone and slanted outward at peculiar angles. Indeed, the moonlight seemed to pour into the white stone cell and blaze off the walls in a fierce brightness. "You shall remain here and be scalded by the moon's light until the moon goes. See how you like that!" Spoorn blasted them with a screech to punctuate her remarks, and the screech, as powerful as a wind, nearly toppled the little Elf Owl.

"And no head ducking. We'll be watching," added Skench.

Gylfie managed to recover her balance and planted her tiny talons firmly on the stone. "Well," she said, "at least we're not plucked."

"Gylfie, are you yoicks?"

"In these situations, Soren, you have to look on the bright side — no pun intended," Gylfie said as she looked around and saw moonlight bouncing off every surface.

"Gylfie, I don't think there is a bright side, pun or not. Plucked or moon scalded? You consider that a choice?"

"We're not going to be either!" A new fierceness had crept into Gylfie's voice.

"Well, how do you think we can avoid it? You can stand in my shadow but it's not exactly as if I can stand in yours — you're a midget."

"That is not fair, Soren, and you know it. Stature jokes are not appropriate. They are considered very bad form where I come from. Indeed, there is a society, the Small Owl Society — SOS — and its charter is to prevent cruel and tasteless remarks concerning size. My grandmother and a Pygmy Owl founded it." Gylfie brimmed with indignation. She seemed far more upset about Soren's use of the word "midget" than being stuck in the white stone chamber for moon scalding.

"I'm sorry. But I still don't see how we're going to avoid the moonlight in here."

"We have to think."

"But that is just what it is impossible to do when one is moon blinked, Gylfie. I think this is it for us." Soren looked down at Gylfie and, even as he said it, he felt a strange numbness stealing over him. And Gylfie's eyes began to blink in an odd manner.

In the blaze of the moon's light, the two young owls felt their essence departing. Soren's brain swam with confusion. His gizzard seemed to grow still. He looked at the moon-blasted walls of the stone cell and they appeared slippery, slippery as ice, and on this ice of the moon's light he felt his memories slip, slip, slipping away. He wanted to grab on to them with his talons, hold them, but he was simply too tired. He was about to fall asleep and when he awoke he knew he would be a changed owl. He would be unrecognizable to himself. He would truly have become 12-1 and Gylfie, too, would no longer be Gylfie but a number, 25-2 — rhymes with Ga'Hoole!

There was a click inside Soren's head. The moment he had thought of the word Ga'Hoole something seemed to clear in his brain. His gizzard stirred. *Ga'Hoole*. The mere mention of the Ga'Hoole legends had made Auntie Finny faint, but the mere thought of the word crashed like thunder and seemed to wake Soren up.

"Gylfie! Gylfie!" He nudged the tiny owl with one of his talons. "Gylfie, have you ever heard of the legends of Ga'Hoole?" Gylfie, whose movements seemed thick and slow, suddenly twitched. Soren could almost see a pulse course through the little owl, jerking her into alertness.

"Ga'Hoole — why, yes. My mother and father would often tell us tales. Tales of Yore we called them."

"We called them legends — the Ga'Hoolian legends." With each mention of the word, the young owls seemed to grow slightly more alert, something within them quickening.

"I think," said Soren, "that we should tell those Tales of Yore until the moon goes down, and maybe these words will thin the full shine and be our shield against this scalding."

Gylfie looked at Soren in wonder. *However did this Barn Owl come upon these ideas?!*

And so Soren began . . .

"Once upon a time, before there were kingdoms of owls, in a time of ever-raging wars, there was an owl born in the country of the Great North Waters and his name was Hoole. Some say there was an enchantment cast upon him at the time of his hatching, that he was given natural gifts of extraordinary power. But what was known of this owl was that he inspired other owls to great and noble deeds and that, although he wore no crown of gold, the owls knew him as a king, for indeed his good grace and conscience anointed him and his spirit was his crown. In a wood of straight tall trees he had hatched, in a glimmering time when the seconds slow between the last minute of the old year and the first of the new, and the forest on this night was sheathed in ice."

Soren's voice was hushed and lovely as he told the tale of the first legend of Ga'Hoole, the "Coming of Hoole." The two little owls' hearts grew strong, their brains cleared, and their gizzards once again quickened.

CHAPTER THIRTEEN

Perfection!

I think it's working," the Screech Owl Spoorn said to the Ablah General, Skench. From their stone perches high above the moon blaze cell, Skench and Spoorn looked down on Soren and Gylfie. They could not hear the hushed tale that Soren was repeating and the two young owls were careful to stand very still. When the moon finally slipped down in the night sky, Skench and Spoorn alighted onto the floor of the moon blaze cell and peered into each of the owl's eyes.

"Perfect!" Spoorn declared.

"We are perfect," Gylfie replied. "We are so pleased to be perfect for our masters. Number 25-2 feels quite perfect and complete."

Soren picked up the cue. "Number 12-1 also feels perfect. We await your commands."

"Come along, little ones. I knew you could do it," Spoorn said. This was the most kindly tone either Soren or Gylfie had ever heard Spoorn use.

"Next thing you know, you'll be having your Special-ness ceremony."

Racdrops! thought Gylfie.

"You know, Spoorn," Skench was saying, "these two were marked as haggards from the start, or at least the Barn Owl was, and sometimes I think that a haggard once scalded actually makes a better servant to our cause."

Dream on, you addle-brained idiot bird. The words roared silently in Soren's head.

"I am thinking of the little one for battle claw mainte-nance and the Barn Owl for the eggorium."

"Or maybe even the hatchery for the little one."

Hatchery! Eggorium! Battle claws! Soren and Gylfie were suddenly very alert. Yet they managed to walk in the dazed manner of the perfectly moon blinked.

"You know," Skench continued, "I think we need to put them in the same stone pit and the same glaucidium — reinforced moon scalding. If they look into each other's eyes, I think it has been proven that it reinforces the ef-fects of the scalding."

Ha! Gylfie nearly laughed out loud.

So the two young owls were returned to Soren's glau-cidium, and Jatt and Jutt were duly informed that these two were to be together and periodically made to gaze into each other's eyes.

"All right, you two!" barked Jutt. "Face off!"

And neither Jatt nor Jutt could see the twinkle deep within each of the young owl's eyes, nor did they hear Soren say, as they turned their backs, "We did it, Gylfie. We did it."

So once more the days slipped into the nights, and the nights became dark links in the silver chain of the moon as it cycled through its dwenkings and full shines, sometimes appearing as an immense, throbbing, bright globe, at other times as thin as the finest thread of down filament from an owl's breast. Patiently, they waited for their flight feathers to grow in. Each day, Soren would do a quick inventory of what he had, what showed promise. His flight feathers were definitely advancing, perhaps not fully fledged, but definitely out there. When he flipped his head back, as owls could do, and rotated it, he could get a good view of his tail feathers, and when no one was looking, he would practice rotating and ruddering maneuvers. There would, of course, be no First Flight ceremonies. In fact, Soren lived in perpetual dread of being informed in a most unceremonious way that he was not "destined" for flight as, apparently, the Spotted Owl, 12-8, formerly Hortense, had been. This, she always said, was due to her top secret status that had something to do with being a broody.

"Think of all we've learned, Soren," Gylfie said one day, after having served in the battle claws chamber. She seemed blithely confident that when the time came for them to fly they would, and that it was much more important to survey the entire range of canyons and gulches that composed St. Aggie's, so that when they were ready they could escape, never be caught again, and warn others. "Let me tell you what I've learned today in the battle claws chamber. . . ."

Soren indulged Gylfie and let her run on. "Well," she began, "they have the battle claws that fit over their talons but they don't make them themselves. They can sort of repair them but basically they have to scavenge them from other places, other battlefields."

"But what other battlefields? Look, Gylfie, I didn't live long in Tyto but I never saw or heard my parents talk about any battles. Did you ever hear your parents talk of any?"

Gylfie thought hard. "No. No, I didn't," she said slowly. "And when we were snatched they weren't wearing them."

"They would hardly need them for us. We were nestlings. Our own talons were not even hardened off." Gylfie blinked at Soren as if he had just said something astonishing. She remained silent for a moment.

"That's just it, isn't it, Soren? They didn't need them for

us. No. But they needed us and these battle claws for something bigger . . . much bigger. Remember in the third legend of the Ga'Hoolian cycle when the sea serpents that could walk upon the land and swim in the sea started to form their plan? Remember how they wanted to drag the entire world of owls and birds into the sea, so that they could reign on both land and sea?"

"Yes," Soren said quietly.

"I think they are planning something big like that."

Soren started to say that the story of the serpents was just a legend and not true, that such sea creatures did not exist. But then he realized deep within himself it didn't really matter. These owls did exist and maybe they wanted just what the imaginary creatures of the legends wanted. Soren had a horrible vision of the entire forest kingdom of Tyto and the desert kingdom of Kuneer and all the owl kingdoms being swirled into this stone world of St. Aggie's.

"So," Gylfie continued, "when we do escape, Soren, we must know as much as we can. We must know about flecks and why they are more precious than gold, and what they plan to do to the kingdoms of owls. It is going to be our duty to warn the rest of the owl kingdoms. Don't worry about flying now. Think about how much we are learning. Look, we know the pelletorium inside out, we've been on cricket detail, now battle claws; the last area we have to crack — pardon the pun — is the eggorium and that broody place."

"Top secret. Remember."

"As if 12-8 would ever let us forget. Oh, Glaux, here she comes now. Hang on, Soren, I'm going to try some of my charm." Gylfie winked and then the dull light of a moon-blinked owl stole into her eyes.

Soren watched as Gylfie, in the semblance of the perfectly moon-blinked owl, trotted up to Hortense. "12-8, you appear calm and satisfied from the perfection of performing your duty well. I cannot imagine that your Specialness ceremony is far off."

"I do not need a ceremony to feel special. For you see, 25-2, I am entrusted with the most sacred and vital of tasks for our beloved St. Aggie's community."

"Yes, that must be so. 12-1 and I would feel it an honor to serve in such a manner. But then again we do not have the qualifications, the obvious talents of you, 12-8. Ah, to be the vessel of such trust."

12-8 seemed to swell with pride before their eyes. A pit monitor suddenly swooped down. "Humbleness correction, humility check, dear." It was a smallish, whiskered

Screech Owl. Her amber eyes blinked a warning out of her bristly face. 12-8 seemed to shrink to half her size instantly. "Oh, I beg your pardon. It is pride in my work, not pride in myself. I remain a humble servant to a great cause."

"Yes, a great cause." Gylfie repeated the words, and although it was a statement, Soren really heard a question at the center. *What was this great cause?*

"Yes, that's better, dear." The whiskered Screech Owl nodded and floated off to a higher perch in the stone pit.

Gylfie felt that the moment was right. "You are the last owl in the world that I would ever say lacked humility, 12-8. You are for my friend and myself a perfect example of humility. You are beyond humbleness! You are . . ." Gylfie was madly searching for a word. *What's she going to say next?* Soren couldn't imagine. He had never seen such a demonstration of outrageous fawning. "You are *subglaucious*." 12-8 blinked at the word as did Soren, who had no idea what *subglaucious* meant. "We, my friend and I, only wish that we could serve in the eggorium and thus attain such humbleness as yourself."

"Your words are kind, 25-2. I shall hope that they might encourage me in my continuing quest for humility while in service to a great cause." She wandered off looking a tad more moon blinked than before, if that was possible.

"What in Glaux's name is *subglaucious?*" Soren said as soon as she was out of earshot.

"No idea. I made it up. We've got to get into that eggorium and the hatchery," Gylfie replied, and the twinkle returned to her eyes.

CHAPTER FOURTEEN

The Eggorium

The following day, Soren was back at his post in the pelletorium. Indeed, he had been promoted to a second-degree picker and was now appalled to find himself reciting the exact same words to a new owlet that 47-2 had said to him upon arriving. "I am 12-1. I am to be your guide for the pelletorium. Follow me." He spoke in the same peculiar manner. The hollow, clipped sounds came naturally to him now. So when Gylfie came up with a tray of fresh pellets, he was perhaps more than ready to listen to her suggestions of a possible new worksite.

"The eggorium. I think I found us an entry-level position. Egg sorting. Fellow in the pellet storage area told me about it. Mite blight in the hatchery."

"So what does that mean?" Soren asked.

"I'm not sure. All I know is that they had to take owls off duty in the eggorium and put them in the hatchery."

"I still don't really understand what they do in either one of those places. Not to mention, what are these flecks that the first-degree pickers pick? It's like a puzzle that never seems to quite come together. It's as if we have all these pieces of things, but are we any closer to knowing what this place is about and how to get out of it, or if we'll ever learn to fly?" Soren was getting more and more agitated as he spoke.

"Try to keep calm, Soren. I just have a feeling that we're close to something."

Soren and Gylfie stood in a small antechamber. Above them perched a large Snowy Owl.

"Welcome to the eggorium!" the Snowy hooted deeply. "To work in the eggorium and the hatchery is the highest of honors. You have been given temporary top secret clearance. We are in a bit of a bind these days as we have had an epidemic of mite blight. For this reason you shall not be given a DNF, or Destined Not to Fly ranking, but you shall have to undergo a procedure at the end of your term, which, although not painful, shall make you forget the information that you shall be exposed to here."

"Moon scalding," Gylfie whispered. "But we know how to handle that."

"Right." Soren was still weak with relief over not being a DNF.

"And now into the eggorium. Please follow me." The Snowy hooted softly.

There was a collective gasp from all the owls. For even a perfectly moon-blinked owl could not help but be stunned by the scene before them. Thousands upon thousands of eggs were being sorted, eggs of all sizes and all pure white, glistening now in the moonlight. And as they sorted, they sang a song.

By these eggs we set a store
We sort them out and ask for more.
Pygmy, Elf, Spotted, and Snowy
Make our gizzards get all glowie.
Barn Owls, Great Grays, Barred, and Screech
Give our hearts an extra beat.

The work's top secret, that is true,
But we are the best — the eggorium crew!
Don't give a hoot that no one flies
For upon these eggs the future relies.
Such is our noble destiny
To guard St. Aggie's through eternity!

The instructions were simple. For this first phase, each of them was to look for eggs of their own species, as these would be the easiest for them to identify. Thus Soren was to sort out Barn Owl eggs and Gylfie was to sort out Elf Owl eggs. They were to roll the eggs into a designated area. From there, they would be transported by larger and more experienced owls to the hatchery.

Soren was simply aghast. This was exactly what he had overheard his mother and father talking about — egg snatching. "Unspeakable!" That was the word his mother had used. *Unspeakable.* But here it was, right before his very eyes. He began to tremble. There was a sickening feeling in his gizzard.

"Don't go yeep on me," Gylfie hissed.

"How can I go yeep? I don't even know how to fly yet."

Going *yeep*, as every owl and bird knew, was a term for when one's wings seemed to lock, when a bird lost its instincts and could no longer fly and would suddenly plummet to the ground.

As loathsome as the work was, it was pretty easy. However, Soren could not help but wonder with each Barn Owl egg he found where it had come from in Tyto. Did his parents know this owl egg's parents? Luckily, the Barn Owl egg station and the Elf Owl station were not that far apart. So as Soren and Gylfie arrived at their respective stations, rolling their eggs, they would exchange a word or two. "I haven't seen 12-8, Hortense," Soren said.

"She's not here. She's in the hatchery. That's where the broodies are — they sit on the eggs. We've got to get in there."

"How do you plan to do that?" Soren asked.

"I don't know. I'll think of something," Gylfie said.

Just before their shift ended, Gylfie thought of something.

"You!"

"Me what?" Soren asked.

"You're a perfect broody."

"What? Me a broody? Have you gone yoicks? I'm a male owl. Male owls don't sit nests."

"They do occasionally — in very cold climates sometimes."

"Well, this isn't an especially cold climate. Why not you?"

"They don't need an Elf Owl now but they do need a Barn Owl. I heard them talking and, by the way, they have plenty of male owls up there sitting on nests."

"What do you mean by 'up there'? Up where?"

"Up there, Soren. I think it's higher than the library. . . ."

I think it's very close to the sky. I think . . ." Gylfie paused for dramatic effect. "We could fly from up there."

Soren felt his gizzard give a lurch. "I'll go!"

"Good fella!" Gylfie gave Soren a friendly cuff, although she was so short she could hardly reach his wing. But it seemed like a really male owl thing to do and she wanted to assure Soren that, although he was going to be a broody, he was still one tough little owl. "And I myself plan on getting promoted to moss tender."

CHAPTER FIFTEEN
The Hatchery

It was Soren's second night on the job. He actually worked a shift with three other Barn Owls, one of whom was male. When it was a night shift, he did not have to report to the glaucidium. It wasn't quite as humiliating as he had thought. There certainly was a constant stream of food. Broodies were well tended. Someone was always coming by, clucking, "How about a nice fat worm, just flown in from Tyto, a bit of snake, a vole, red squirrel." No, the eating was definitely good in the hatchery. Gylfie did manage to get herself in as a moss tender. And if their shifts coincided, there was plenty of time to talk, as Gylfie made extra trips to tuck moss and bits of fluff into Soren's nest. Soren had four eggs in his nest, which seemed a tad crammed. He thought mostly there were two or three eggs to a Barn Owl's nest. But then again, what did he know? Just as he was beginning to think on this, the second night, that it wasn't so bad, the Barn Owl on the nest next to him spoke in that empty moon-blinked voice, "Crack alert! Crack alert. Egg tooth visible."

Two Barred Owls came hustling over. Soren felt his gizzard twinge with excitement. He leaned out of his nest to take a peek. The egg was giving those familiar shudders — just like Eglantine's egg had, which now seemed so long ago. But no one seemed at all excited. No one was gasping with joy, saying, "It's coming! It's coming!"

The egg was rocking now. Soren could see the little hole and the egg tooth, pale and glistening, poking out.

"All right," said the first Barred Owl in a cool voice. "Enough with that egg tooth. Let's crack it." And with that, the two Barred Owls gave solid thwacks with their talons. The egg split. Then one of the Barred Owls hooked the slimy white blob with its talon and firmly pulled it out while the other one turned the shell up. "Bottoms up!" the owl said crisply, and she dumped out the hatchling.

Soren was so shocked he could barely breathe. No one exclaimed "It's a girl!" No one said "adorable" or "enchanting." No one said anything except "Number 401-2."

The other Barred Owl nodded in response. "So we're into the four hundred sequence with the Barn Owls, now."

"Yes, what an accomplishment," sighed the one who had numbered this little owlet. Soren felt a rage. Accomplishment! This was the most horrid, despicable thing he had ever witnessed. A coldness that began in his gizzard seemed to creep through Soren from his new tail feathers up to his wing tips and down to his talons. He realized that he would rather see this little owl dead than alive in St. Aggie's. They had to get out. He and Gylfie had to get out. They must learn to fly. Where was Gylfie? She was on this shift. He wished she could come by and see this. He craned his head about but there was no sign of the little Elf Owl.

It was the stillest time of the moonless night, and on break Gylfie had stepped into a large crack in the rock, perfect for hiding an Elf Owl. She was watching Hortense. Hortense had proven herself to be such an exceptional broody that she had been given a big nest on a large out-cropping of stone somewhat away from the others, where there was more room. She had become very adept at spreading herself over several eggs at a time. It was a change in shift for moss tenders in Gylfie's area so it would be a while before any came by.

And now the Spotted Owl, who was indeed large for an owl her age, was doing something rather odd. She had actually stepped off her nest, and it appeared to Gylfie as if she were trying to dislodge an egg from the nest. Gylfie blinked and blinked again. Gylfie nearly gasped out loud as she saw 12-8 gently roll the egg to the edge of the stone outcropping. Then, out of the blackness of this moonless night, there appeared a spot of dazzling white — just a spot like a tiny moon floating in the darkness, a tiny feathered moon! Gylfie's eyes widened. It was the head of a bald eagle. She had seen them in the desert. This one was huge and had a wingspan that was immense. It alighted on the ledge and silently picked up the egg in its talons. Not a word was exchanged. Indeed, the only thing that Gylfie heard was a soft sigh in the night as 12-8 climbed back on her nest.

Gylfie and Soren finally met up at dawn when they were both due to go off their shifts. They each were so eager to talk about their experiences that they began to argue as to who would go first. Finally, Gylfie hissed her news. "12-8! She's an infiltrator!"

"What?" Soren was stunned. His beak dropped open. The story of the horrific hatching seemed like nothing compared to this.

"A spy," Gylfie said in a throaty voice.

"Wait. Are we talking about the same owl? Hortense? Number 12-8?"

"She's no more 12-8 than I'm 25-2 or you're — what's your number? I keep forgetting."

"12-1," Soren said dimly. "Hush, here she comes now."

Hortense walked by and then stopped. "I hear, number 12-1, that you are doing an admirable job as a broody. It is the most rewarding work. Each little egg that I bring to hatching makes me feel satisfied in a most humble way."

"Thank you, 12-8," Soren replied numbly. Then the Spotted Owl turned to Gylfie: "And I understand that you are an excellent moss tender. You, too, might advance to become a broody for small eggs. I am sure you shall find complete fulfillment in this task."

Gylfie nodded mutely.

What an actress!

For the next two nights, Soren and Gylfie argued about how they would confront Hortense.

"I think we should just go up to her when she's alone," Gylfie said. "And we say, 'Hortense, it has come to our attention . . .'"

"What do you mean 'come to our attention'? You spied on her, Gylfie. That could make her nervous, 'the come to our attention' bit. She might think a lot of owls have seen her."

"You're right."

"Why do we have to confront her at all?"

"Why? Well, what if she's part of something here?

What if there are twenty Hortenses in St. Aggie's? What if there is some hidden network of . . . of disgruntled un-moon-blinked owls? Maybe they're planning a revolution."

"What's a revolution?" Soren asked, and Gylfie blinked.

"It's kind of like war but the sides aren't exactly equal. It's like the little fellows rising up against the big baddies," Gylfie said.

"Oh," said Soren.

"Look," Gylfie said, "we have to make friends, real friends, with Hortense. Her nest is in the highest place in St. Aggie's. That's where we're going to leave from." Gylfie paused and walked right under Soren's beak. "Look down at me, Soren."

"What?"

"Soren, we've got to learn how to fly. Now!"

CHAPTER SIXTEEN
Hortense's Story

But first, they had to talk to Hortense. It was not, of course, just a question of picking the right moment but the right words. The moment was easy enough. The following evening, Soren and Gylfie managed to synchronize their schedules so that Soren had a break from his broody chores while Gylfie was still on moss-tending duty. Soren requested permission to help his friend deliver moss, which was granted, as there were still shortages in both the hatchery and the eggorium. Together, the two owls made their way up to the distant outcropping where Hortense sat this evening on a large nest with at least eight eggs in it.

"Phew!" Soren sighed. "Some hike up here."

"Nothing to it." Gylfie hopped along. "You get used to it. All right, now, you know the drill. You begin."

It was Soren who had thought of the opening words — or word. The opening word was a name: "Hortense." And the speech was simple.

They were now approaching the top of the outcrop. The wind was strong. Indeed, it was the first time that Soren had felt the wind since he had arrived at St. Aggie's. Silvery dark clouds raced against the sky. This was where owls belonged — up high with the wind and the sky and the stars that swirled in the night. He felt invigorated and confident.

"Welcome 25-2 and 12-1 to my humble abode."

Soren dropped the moss from his beak onto the nest, and Hortense began tucking it into the niches and gaps. "Hortense!"

Hortense looked up and blinked at him. Her yellow eyes thickened with the moon-blink gaze.

"Hortense, this is not humble, this is where owls belong — high, near the wind, near the sky, close to the heartbeat of the night." *Amazing*, Gylfie thought. Soren might not know the word "revolution" but this owl could talk. "Hortense, you are an owl, a Spotted Owl."

"I am number 12-8."

"No you're not, Hortense," Soren said, and this was Gylfie's cue.

"Hortense, cut the pellets. You are Hortense and I saw you acting not as 12-8 but as Hortense, the brave, imaginative Spotted Owl. I saw you deliver an egg from this nest to an eagle."

At that moment, Hortense blinked again and the daze lifted from her eyes, simply evaporated like fog on a sunny day. "You saw?"

"I saw, Hortense," Gylfie said gently. "You are no more moon blinked than we are."

"I had my suspicions about you two," Hortense said softly. Her eyes seemed to lose their brittle stare. Indeed, Soren thought they were the loveliest owl eyes he had ever seen. Deep brown like the still pool in the forest that he had seen from his family's nest in the fir tree. But there was also a kind of flickering light in them. Speckles of white dotted the crown of her head and her entire body seemed dappled in shades of amber and brown, shot through with spots of white like blurry stars.

"We never suspected you," Soren added quickly. "That is, until Gylfie saw you that night."

"Are there any other owls here that are un-moon blinked?" Gylfie asked.

"We're the only three, I think."

"How did you get here? How did you resist moon blinking?"

"It's a long story how I got here. And, as to how I resisted moon blinking, well, I'm not sure. You see, where I come from there is a stream, and the flecks that they pick from pellets run heavily in that stream."

"What are the flecks?" Gylfie asked.

"I'm not sure of that, either. They can be found in rocks and soil and water. They seem to occur everywhere, but in our part of the Kingdom of Ambala there is a large deposit that runs through the creeks and rivers. It is both a blessing and a curse. Some of us have unusual powers because of the flecks, we think, but for others it disrupts their navigational abilities to fly true courses. I had a grandmother who eventually lost her wits entirely, but before that she hatched my father, who could see through rock."

"What? Impossible!"

"No, it's true, yet my brother went blind at an early age. So one never knew how it might affect them. I think in my case it perhaps made me resistant to moon blinking. But that doesn't explain how I got here. It was no accident. I chose to come."

"You chose to come?" Gylfie and Soren both gasped.

"I told you it's a long story."

"I'm on break," Soren said.

"And they're short on monitors. I won't be missed," Gylfie added.

"Well, first of all, I am much older than I appear. I am a fully mature owl."

"What?!" Soren and Gylfie both said with complete disbelief.

"Yes, it's true. I hatched almost four years ago."

"Four years ago!" Soren said.

"Yes, indeed, but perhaps one of the effects of the flecks on me was that I was always small, small as an owlet, and never really grew to be much bigger than owlet size. My feathers were delayed coming in, and, of course, I have further delayed them." At this point, Hortense stuck her beak into the nest and pulled out a lovely brown-and-white Spotted Owl feather.

"Is that from a molt?" Soren asked. He had molted when he had shed his first down. There had been a First Molting ceremony, and his mother had saved those baby feathers in a special place.

"No, not a molt. I pull them out myself."

"You pluck yourself?!" Soren and Gylfie gasped in horror.

"Well," she laughed, and the *churr* sound of a Spotted Owl's laughter was indeed a lovely sound that no moonblinked owl could ever make. "I am," she said with a twinkle in her eye, "a DNF."

"Destined Not to Fly." Soren said the words softly.

"Yes, because of my top secret work, but also because of my delayed feather development. So I was a natural."

"A natural for what?" Gylfie asked.

"To come here. To find out what was going on. You see,

in the Forest of Ambala, our losses due to St. Aggie's patrols had become increasingly heavy. We had been losing baby owlets and eggs at an astonishing rate. Something had to be done. And this, of course, meant sacrifices. One of our bravest owls had followed a St. Aggie's patrol and discovered this maze of stone canyons in which they lived. That particular owl, Cedric, had sacrificed an egg from his and his mate's nest just so he could follow them.

"I volunteered for service as well. I figured that I probably wouldn't have much of a normal life, what with my delayed feather development, and then when my feathers finally did come in, they just didn't seem to work that well. No power, no lift, shaky drag capabilities. I could hardly manage anything but the shortest of flights. Who would have me as a mate? What kind of mother would I make, not being able to hunt or teach my babies to fly? How should I put it? I was bound to be one of those odd single owls, always dependent on relatives' charity, given the wormy, maggoty, down-the-trunk hollow. I hated the idea of being the pathetic dependent owl, the one the owlets were always forced to visit. I decided that it was contrary to my nature to lead such a life and that if I could not live like a normal owl, I would, in fact, use my disability for some noble purpose. Thus, I chose to go to St. Aggie's and do whatever I could to stop them in their horrible quest for power and control of the kingdoms of owls. For that is what they want to do. You realize this, don't you?"

Soren and Gylfie nodded numbly.

"The eggs are part of it. I do what I can here. Since my arrival I have saved more than twenty eggs. The owls of Ambala work with the big bald eagles. It's safest that way. Eagles can get closest to this place most freely. Rock crevices are the natural nesting places for many eagles. So they know the territory. The eagle is the one bird that really strikes fear into the gizzard of these owls. That scar on Skench's wing — that was the talon work of an eagle."

"But how did you get here if you can't fly long distances?" Soren asked.

"HALO," Hortense replied.

"HALO?" Gylfie and Soren both said at once.

"High Altitude Low Opening situation. You see, you wait for a day with thick cloud cover. I had plucked myself to owlet status." Soren winced. "Two big Snowies who blended in perfectly with the cloud cover flew me to the boulders just before the entrance of the canyons of St. Aggie's. There is a grove of trees there with a lot of moss under them. It's where the moss that is used in these nests comes from. No owls live there anymore but that is where they dropped me on that cloudy day."

"You say you've saved twenty eggs?"

"Yes, indeed. And back in Ambala they now tell stories of me. I, who had no stories, am now the hero of stories," Hortense said with no pretense of humility.

"But Hortense," Soren said, "there must be more to your life than this. You cannot remain here forever."

"The eagles promise to come and get me. But I always say, 'oh, just another dozen more or so.' I have become rather addicted to what I am doing."

"But there are risks," Gylfie said.

"Anything worth doing has risks." Hortense paused. "And believe me, this is worth doing."

"We want to get out of here. Won't you come with us?" Soren said.

"How can I? I can't fly. Nor can you, for that matter."

"But we're going to learn," Soren said fiercely.

"Good," Hortense replied softly, and there was a quaver in her voice that gave both Soren and Gylfie a very creepy feeling. Then, realizing that perhaps she had frightened them, Hortense spoke cheerfully. "Oh, don't worry. I am sure you shall. Where there's a wing there's a way! Now let me see those wings of yours."

Gylfie and Soren both spread their wings for Hortense to examine. "Lovely, lovely," she said softly. "Coverts coming in nicely, Soren. Very nice tip slots developing between the primaries. Essential for drag control, especially during turbulent conditions. Your barbs, both of you, are still soft but they'll stiffen up. And I am sure you will both make splendid fliers."

"Any chance we could see the eagles when they come in?" Soren asked.

"Well . . . they fly in just before first light."

"I'll work a double shift so I can come up here," Gylfie said quickly. "And Soren, try to arrange for a break then for yourself."

CHAPTER SEVENTEEN
Save the Egg!

"Number 32-9 reporting for broody duty." An extremely large Barn Owl stood at the edge of the nest. Soren scrambled down and set off to find Gylfie. He met her on the rubbly path leading up to the outcropping where Hortense was.

"You realize, of course," Soren was saying as the winds began to buffet them on their ascent, "that when we learn to fly, the outcropping will make the ideal takeoff spot. Always a breeze to bounce you up. Perfect."

By the time they arrived, Hortense already had the egg out of the nest and was pushing it toward the edge of the rock.

"Can we help?" Soren asked.

"Thank you both, but it is really better if I do it by myself. The fewer birds to touch this egg, the less confused the hatchling will be when it comes out."

"Ah, here she comes. No mate with her tonight again. Must be busy elsewhere," Hortense said. "Gives me such a thrill every time I spot those wings. Magnificent, aren't they?"

Soren saw the white head, brighter than any star, melt from the dim pearly gray of the dawn. The immensity of the eagle wings was incredible. Soren was enraptured. So enraptured that he didn't hear Gylfie's desperate hiss. Finally, a sharp beak poked him in the knees.

"Soren, quick! I hear someone coming up the path." Then Soren heard it, too. Gylfie dived into a narrow slot. The slot was much too skinny for a fat Barn Owl like Soren.

"Come in. Come in. We'll squeeze up. It's wider inside." Gylfie was desperate and Soren was nearly frozen with fear to the rock beneath his talons. When owls are frightened, their feathers lie flat and they do become slimmer. So, with fear pumping through him, Soren indeed seemed to shrink. He pressed himself into the crack that, in fact, did widen as it deepened in the rock. He hoped he was not crushing Gylfie. They both were barely breathing as the horrifying scene began to unfold on the outcropping.

"12-8!" The screech seemed to crack the sky. *Good Glaux, it was Skench and Spoorn and Jatt and Jutt. And Auntie!* Auntie puffed and angry, the yellow light from her eyes no longer soft but a hard metallic glare.

"I suspected her for some time!" Auntie squawked, and

dragged Hortense off the nest that she had just moments before returned to.

The egg, limned by the rising sun, stood fragile and quivering at the edge of the rock. Soren's eyes were riveted on the egg. The egg loomed so large, so fragile against the dawn sky. *It could have been Eglantine. It could have been Eglantine.* The thought began to swell in Soren's brain and fill him with a profound terror. This was the future they were fighting for. This was the evilness of St. Aggie's. The egg teetered on the brink as did the entire world of owls. The eagle hovered above.

Suddenly, there was a deep mournful howl. "Go for the egg! Don't worry about me. Save the egg . . . save the egg!" Hortense shrieked. Then a huge shadow slid across the outcropping and next there was an explosion of feathers. It seemed to Soren that there was nothing but feathers. Feathers and down everywhere swirling in the glimmering rosy light of the new day. The eagle was everyplace at once. And Hortense's voice kept crying, "Save the egg! Save the egg!" Auntie was the fiercest fighter of them all. Her beak open and ready to tear, her yellow eyes flashing madly in her head, her talons extended and trying to rip at the eagle's eyes, she was a white squall of fury. Scalding curses tore from her mouth. "Kill! Kill!" she screamed in a high-pitched deafening voice. Her feathered-face hardened until it seemed like stone. Slashed by a dark beak and the savage yellow eyes, it was a blazing white mask of brutality.

Then Gylfie and Soren saw the eagle take a mighty swipe with her wings and send Auntie tumbling flat on her back. In that moment, the eagle reached the egg and rose into the sky with it clutched in her claws.

Yet the voice of Hortense seemed to grow dimmer, as if it was fading away, dwindling as if . . . as if . . . Soren and Gylfie looked at each other. Two big tears leaked from Soren's dark eyes. "She's falling, isn't she, Gylfie?"

"They pushed her." And there was Auntie, standing at the edge of the cliff with Spoorn, looking down into the thousand-foot-deep abyss. "Bye-bye," Auntie cooed, and waved a tattered wing. "Bye-bye, 12-8, you fool!" The coo curled into the ugliest snarl Soren could ever imagine.

"But the eagle got the egg," Gylfie said weakly.

"Yes, I suppose she did," Soren replied.

And now there would be more stories, indeed, legends to tell in Ambala of brave Hortense.

The eggorium was briefly shut down. All temporary eggorium and hatchery owls were to report to the moon-blaze chamber immediately for moon scalding, as indeed there was to be a full shine the following evening. Soren and Gylfie, still crammed in the slot, heard Auntie and Spoorn and Skench talking about how no word of this could get out. Auntie's old voice returned. She fretted in that Auntie way of hers about how she could not imagine that 12-8, the most beautifully moon-blinked owl ever, could have gone so wrong under her guidance.

Once again, Gylfie and Soren survived the moon scalding in the moon-blaze chamber. They told the Tales of Yore, as Gylfie called the Ga'Hoolian legends. And Soren, who had a remarkable gift for storytelling, began to compose a new one that first night that he told in bits through the glare of the moon's hot light.

"She was an owl like none other . . ." Soren began, thinking of Hortense. "Her face both beautiful and kindly, her deep brown eyes warm and with a glimmer like tiny suns. Her wings, however, for one reason or another were crippled, and it was from this, her weakness, that she drew her great strength. For this was an owl who wanted only to do good, who clung to dreams of freedom while giving up her own and, from a stony perch high in a lawless place, she did find a way to wage her own war."

Soren finished the legend as the scalding moon began to slip down in the sky.

CHAPTER EIGHTEEN
One Bloody Night

It was the last night of the dwenking. The moon this night appeared like a fragile dim thread in the sky. The last full shine in which they had been moon scalded after their work in the eggorium had seemed the longest. But Soren and Gylfie had survived. Soren poked his beak into the feathers, the very feathers that Hortense had said were coming along so nicely. They seemed even thicker now.

"Look at those primaries, Soren, and your plummels! How I do envy your plummels," Gylfie said.

Soren ran his beak lightly through the plummels that hovered like a fine mist over his flight feathers. He remembered his mother saying how one must preen their plummels every day, for, indeed, plummels were unique to owls. Of all birds, only owls, and only certain owls at that, had plummels. Elf Owls did not have these fine, soft feathers that fringed the leading edges of wings. It was these feathers that allowed Barn Owls like Soren to fly in almost complete silence.

"Plummels," his mother had said, "are every bit as important as a sharp beak or sharp talons." These words, of course, were directed mostly to Kludd. Kludd's plummels had just begun to sprout shortly before Soren had been snatched, but all Kludd cared about was his beak and talons."

"So, Gylfie, you think, then, by the time of the next dwenking we shall be able to leave?"

"Yes."

Soren looked at this little owl who had become his friend and felt a twinge. She could leave now, for Gylfie was a fully fledged owl. With her dappled plumage of reddish browns and grays and the striking white feathers that curved over her eyes in lovely sweeping arcs, Gylfie looked so grown up, so ready to fly. "Gylfie," Soren sighed, "you could leave now. Look at you."

Gylfie had, indeed, turned into a very lovely Elf Owl. "We have had this talk before, Soren. I told you. I am waiting."

"I know. I know. I just want you to be sure." Soren bobbed his head up and down twice and then cocked it to the side in a questioning manner.

"We still haven't gotten into the library and I feel —"

Soren began to interrupt. For the life of him, he could not figure out why Gylfie was so set on getting into the library. The flecks were interesting but he didn't see how this was connected with anything that had to do with their escaping. The library, of course, was located in a higher part of the canyon, one closer to the sky. Their chances of getting into the hatchery since the Hortense disaster, which would have afforded them the best take-off spot, were absolute zero. And now that was just what Gylfie was saying. "I just feel it in my gizzard, Soren. If we can get into the library, that might be our way out. But until Grimble comes back, I don't think there's a chance."

"Why didn't we think of asking Hortense about Grimble being imperfectly moon blinked?" Soren wondered aloud.

"I doubt if she would have known anything. All she ever saw of this place was the hatchery, really."

"I suppose you're right," Soren replied. "But Gylfie, what's the sense of us getting into the library, even if the library is the second-best escape route, if we can't fly? You said we have to learn and we'd better start quickly. Do we know the first thing about flying except what we remember our parents saying? How can we practice branching here? Start hopping around and trying to do any of the usual things owl chicks have been doing by the time they are our age to be flight-ready, and you'll see the monitors on us faster than if we had asked a question."

"You're right, Soren. We're not ready. We have to figure out a way to practice."

"I'm not sure that we can. I mean, it just seems too risky."

But Gylfie saw that, in fact, Soren was practicing in a very subtle way as they munched their evening ration of crickets in the glaucidium. The Barn Owl had spread his wings and fluffed them up and, although not hopping, Soren had certainly assumed what was known as a flight-prime position. He turned now to 47-2, their pelletorium guide from the first day, and in Gylfie's mind the most perfectly moon-blinked creature of St. Aggie's.

"Just getting the feel of it," Soren said to 47-2. Naturally, he did not wait for 47-2 to ask, "The feel of what?" He merely went ahead and answered his own question in hopes of provoking 47-2 to offer some information. "It must feel wonderful when you finally lift off." He raised his wings slightly as he spoke. "It is almost as if I know exactly where the air will pouch beneath my wings."

"Oh, yes." 47-2 blinked. "That feeling will pass." 47-2's wings hung limply at her sides. "I remember when I had it as well. You won't be bothered much longer with such feelings." She stared straight ahead, her eyes vacant.

Bothered? Why would such feelings ever be a bother? Soren

dared not ask. He could see that Gylfie had heard this as well and was equally disturbed. A dread began to creep up from their gizzards and seep into their hollow bones. They had thought that DNFs, owls Destined Not to Fly, were only those owls who worked in the hatchery and the eggorium. Were there DNFs in the pelletorium as well?

"Yes, yes," 47-2 spoke in her odd flat tones, "it will pass, not much longer, and it is a lovely feeling that comes as they relieve you of those stirrings of flight."

Soren could hardly steady his voice to form the next statement. "Yes, stirrings of flight. I very much like these stirrings of flight. They feel so lovely under my wings."

"No, no. They become more bothersome, trust me. You will welcome the bats when they come."

Bats? *Bats?* Soren and Gylfie desperately needed to know about the bats. How could he wheedle this information out? "I have not seen any bats around here," Soren said, trying to keep the anxiousness out of his voice.

"Oh, they only come just before every other newing or so. To relieve us of flight urges. You are still not ready, I'm afraid. You will have to wait until the next newing."

A hundred questions battered Soren's brain. But 47-2 continued. "They come tonight, I hear. I am very happy in anticipation. It is so lovely. We always sleep our best after the bats quank."

Just at that moment, Jatt and Jutt screeched a call for attention. "All 40's through 48's shall report on the third sleep march to area three." They spoke in unison.

"Hooray!" The cheer welled up in the glaucidium. "Hooray, hooray!" 47-2 danced a strange little jig.

Two marches had gone by. The silver thread of a moon was drawn down to the edge where the sky meets the earth. A last feeble blink of silver and it was gone. The sky grew blacker and blacker. A third sleep march would seem meaningless, for all was engulfed in shadows, and yet the shriek came. Soren and Gylfie moved, following 47-2, but stopped at the edge of area three.

"Look!" Gylfie said. "Look at what they are doing." Soren and Gylfie both stared in disbelief as hundreds of owls flung themselves flat onto their backs with their breasts exposed to the sky and their wings spread out.

"Never," Soren said, "have I seen an owl perch that way. It looks as if it might hurt."

"I don't think it's called perching," Gylfie said. "I think its called lying down."

"Lying down? Animals do that, not birds, and never owls." Soren hesitated. "Not unless they're dead."

But these owls were not dead.

"Listen!" Soren said.

The sky high above the glaucidium seemed suddenly

to pulse with a throbbing sound. It was the sound of wing beats but not the soft, almost silent, wing beats of owls. Instead, there was a tough leathery *snap*. A strange song began to rise in the glaucidium. Then, blacker than the blackness of the night, printed against the sky, ten thousand bats flew overhead as the owls called to them in an odd wailing lament.

Come to us and quackle and quank.
Relieve us of our stirrings
With your fangs so sharp and bright
Take this blood that's always purring.
Through our hollow bones it flows
To each feather and downy fluff.
Quell the terrible, horrid urge that so often prinkles us,
Still our dreams, make slow our thoughts
Let tranquillity flood our veins.
Come to us and drink your fill
So we might end our pains.

Soren and Gylfie watched in unblinking wonder as the vampire bats fluttered down. Using their tiny wing-thumbs and feet, they began to crawl up onto the owls' breasts. They seemed to forage for a few seconds, seeking out a bare spot on the owls' breasts. With gleaming sharp teeth they made a quick tiny cut. The bats' tongues, narrow and grooved, slipped into the nicks. The owls did not even flinch but seemed merely to sigh into the night. Soren and Gylfie were transfixed and could not move. 47-2 turned her head toward them, her eyes half shut, a mild, contented expression on her face.

"That must hurt terribly," Soren spoke softly.

"No, lovely, lovely. The stirrings go. No more . . ." Her voice dwindled into the darkness of the night.

Soren and Gylfie were not sure how long the vampire bats were there, but, indeed, they seemed to swell before their eyes. And then they appeared so gorged, it was as if they staggered rather than lifted into flight. The moon had vanished now for days. The grayness of a new dawn began to filter through the black and, in drunken spirals, the bats wheeled through the remnants of the night.

CHAPTER NINETEEN
To Believe

Ever since that bloody night, Soren and Gylfie had thought of nothing but flying. It had become abundantly clear to them why none of the owlets of St. Aggie's had the sleek glossy feathers or any of the fluffy down of normal owls who had grown beyond the chick stage. Growing flight feathers for an owl was normally not a complicated business, but deprived of the blood supply, these feathers from the primaries to the plummels would wither and die. With that, stirrings, dreams of flight, notions of skyful joy and freedom shriveled and died as well.

Soren and Gylfie's mission was unmistakable: They must learn how to fly despite lacking any opportunity to ever branch, or hop, or practice for flight in any way. They must keep the dream of flight alive in their minds. They must feel it in their gizzards and in that way they would learn to fly. Gylfie repeated the words of her father to Soren: "He said, Soren, that 'you can practice forever and still never fly if you don't believe.' So it's not just practice,

Soren. We must believe, and we can because we are not moon blinked."

"But moon blinked or not, we have to have feathers. And I am still short of flight feathers," Soren replied.

"You are going to have them. You will have enough by the next newing."

"Well, that's just the problem. That's when the vampire bats come back."

Gylfie looked at Soren gravely. "That is why we must learn how to fly before the next newing."

"But I won't be ready. I won't have enough feathers," Soren said.

"Almost, though."

"Almost? There's a difference, Gylfie, between almost and enough."

"Yes. The difference is belief, Soren. Belief." The little Elf Owl said the last word so fiercely that Soren took a step back. "You have a large and generous gizzard, Soren. You feel. I know this. You feel strongly. If any owl can do this, you can."

Soren blinked in dismay. How could he not believe it if this owl, who weighed no more than a wad of leaves, believed so much. It was Gylfie who had the enormous gizzard, not himself.

So the two little owls began to think constantly about

flying. They discussed it whenever they could. They shared memories of their parents lifting out of their nests into the sky. They argued about wing angles and drift and updrafts and a dozen other things they had seen and almost felt as they had watched other owls. They pondered endlessly the stony maze of the canyons and ravines that made up St. Aggie's. They knew that the only way out was straight up, requiring the most difficult of flight maneuvers, especially now that they had no access to Hortense's stone outcropping high in the hatchery. There could be no gradual glide for a takeoff.

Still, they knew that when they escaped, it was essential to find the highest point possible, the point closest to the sky. And Gylfie continued to feel deep in her gizzard that the library would offer such a place, and that within the library they would discover the secret of the flecks, and in some way this secret would become vital to their escape.

One unseasonably warm day, Gylfie had returned to their station in the pelletorium from a run for new pellets. She was barely able to conceal her excitement. "He's back," she whispered to Soren. "Grimble's back! Get on the next shift with me for new pellets."

That would be easy. It was a snack shift, and if you were

on a new pellet run you missed the snack. So no one ever really wanted to go.

Just as the sun reached its high point, Soren and Gylfie stopped walking forward in the Big Crack. They, of course, continued to move their feet as if they were still marching, and the stream of owlets parted around them and moved on as they remained in the same place. Soren blinked. He did not have to look up to feel the piece of blue sky flowing above them. He had passed this point on the trail many times now, and each time he felt refreshed by the very thought of this small wedge of sky so close. He would close his eyes and feel it. When all the owlets had passed, Gylfie gave the signal and they turned down the smaller crack toward the library.

Gylfie marched ahead. Soren was trembling with fear. What if Gylfie's suspicions about Grimble being imperfectly moon blinked were wrong? What if Grimble sounded an alarm? What if they were both seized for the next laughter therapy session? Soren winced and felt a twinge flicker from his down fluff to his brand-new primaries.

Grimble stood in front of the opening to the library. There seemed to be no other owls about. Soren, however, felt the air stir and suddenly realized that it was a breeze. A wonderful thrill coursed through him as it had when he was on the stone outcropping of Hortense's nest. Grimble now turned and blinked at them. Then commenced one of the strangest conversations Soren had ever heard.

"So you are here," Grimble said.

"So we are," replied Gylfie.

"You are conducting yourselves in a dangerous manner," the Boreal Owl said carefully.

"Our lives are not worth two pellets here. We have nothing to lose," Gylfie replied.

"Brave words."

"Not so brave. Wait until you hear my questions. Then you'll know I am brave."

Soren nearly fainted. How could Gylfie even say the word!

Grimble began to shake almost uncontrollably. "You dare say the Q."

"Yes, and I am going to say the *what*, the *when*, and the *why*, and every other word of a free and un-moon-blinked owl. For we are like you, Grimble."

Grimble began to gag. "Whhh-what?"

"What am I talking about? Is that what you wanted to ask? Say it, Grimble. Ask how I know this. Ask anything you want and I'll tell you with one answer: I feel it in my gizzard."

"Gizzard?" Grimble's face grew dreamy with memory.

"Yes. Gizzard, Grimble. Ours still work. And we know, we sense it — that you are not moon blinked. You're faking it just as we are."

"Not completely." The owl blinked. A thin transparent eyelid swept across his eye. Soren knew about these winking eyelids. His parents had told him that when he began to fly, he would find them useful, for they would keep his eyes clear in flight and protect them from any airborne bits of debris. But Grimble was not in flight. No, Grimble was hardly moving. So why was his wink lid flickering madly? Then Soren noticed huge tears gathering at the far corners of his large yellow eyes. "Oh, if only I were perfectly moon blinked. If only I were —"

"Why, Grimble?" Soren asked softly. "Why?"

"I cannot tell you right now. I shall come to you tonight in the glaucidium. I shall arrange for a pass for you. They won't mind as it is now the time of the newing. But let me tell you right now, what you are doing is terribly dangerous. What you are doing could invite a fate much worse than death."

"Worse than death?" Gylfie asked. "What could be worse than death? We would rather die."

"The life I live is worse than death, I assure you."

CHAPTER TWENTY
Grimble's Story

I thought I was being so smart," Grimble said. He had led them into another crack in the canyon wall that was off the large one that led from the pelletorium. "You see, the snatching patrols had just snatched one of my young ones as I was returning with my mate from hunting. It was little Bess. She was my favorite, I have to admit. I swooped in and attacked ferociously. It was actually a cousin of Jatt and Jutt who had Bess in his talons. His name was Ork. He was considered very dangerous and, well, I killed him. The other owls were stunned. They shrank back from me, but then Spoorn and Skench flew in. They saw what had happened. Oddly enough, they were thrilled that Ork was dead. You see, the previous leader of St. Aegolius had died the year before and since then a bitter power struggle had gone on between Ork and his forces and those of Spoorn and Skench. Skench and Spoorn were so happy that they said they would spare my family, never come by our nest again, if I would agree to return to St. Aegolius and join them. They wanted me for my fighting skills. I had killed Ork with no battle claws at all, just my bare talons and beak. They needed me.

"Well, it seemed that there was no choice. I looked at my dear mate. There were three other young ones in the nest. I had to do it. I had to go. My mate begged me not to. She swore that we could go elsewhere, far away. But Skench and Spoorn laughed and said they would find us no matter where we went. So I joined them. My mate and our owlets promised they would never forget me. Spoorn and Skench promised that I could visit them thrice yearly, which, at the time, seemed very generous. I should have suspected something right away. But I didn't know about moon blinking then, either. The visits would become meaningless if I were successfully moon blinked. My family would not recognize me nor would I have any feeling for them. This is because moon-blinked owls have no real feelings, and without our feelings we become unrecognizable over time to those who do have feelings. That is the evil genius of moon blinking.

"So I was determined, like you, to resist and to pretend. I was fairly successful. Skench and Spoorn had valued my fighting skills so much that they allowed me to earn a

name. I had been number 28-5. But I became Grimble."
And now . . ." Grimble began to shake again. "Something
has changed."

"What do you mean? You resisted," Soren said.

"Yes, to a point."

"To a point? You either are or you're not moon blinked,"
Gylfie said.

"After every few newings, we are required even as mature owls to be reblinked. I think something has begun to
change. It seems that although I resisted, now I am losing
something. The faces of my dear mate, my little Bess, have
begun to fade. When I used to visit them, my old voice
came back. The call of Boreal Owls is like a song, some say
like the bells that used to toll in the churches, but now it
has become flat. Eight or so newings ago, when I made one
of my visits home, I called out as usual as I approached,
but no one recognized my call. Then two newings ago,
when I arrived, neither my mate nor Bess recognized me."

"Unbelievable," Gylfie whispered.

"And now they are gone," Grimble said.

"Gone?" said Soren. "You mean they left?"

"They left, or perhaps they were killed by Skench and
Spoorn or perhaps . . ." Grimble's voice dwindled off.

"Perhaps what?" Gylfie pressed.

"Perhaps they are there and I simply cannot see them

at all, nor do they recognize me. I think I have become like air — transparent, like nothingness. Is that not the ultimate savagery of being moon blinked? I would say that in another few newings I shall be the perfectly moon-blinked elderly owl."

"But why? Why do they do this? What is the purpose of St. Aggie's?" Soren asked.

"And the flecks, what are they about?" Gylfie looked straight up at the Boreal Owl, who towered over her.

"Ah! One simple question, one not quite so simple. The purpose of St. Aggie's is to take control of every owl kingdom on Earth."

"And to destroy it?" asked Soren.

"You can be sure the kingdoms shall be destroyed, but control is really what they want. And for the kind of control they want they must moon blink. That is their main tool, for moon blinking destroys will, erases individuality, makes everyone the same. The flecks, however, are another kind of tool, a weapon for war."

"What can flecks do?" Gylfie asked.

"No one really knows. I am not entirely sure. The flecks do have powers if certain things are done to them."

"What kind of powers?"

"Again, I am not certain. They seem to be able to pull things toward them, sometimes. When I am working in the fleck storage area of the library, sometimes I think I can feel their force."

Soren and Gylfie were mystified. "How strange," Gylfie said.

"Teach us to fly, Grimble! Teach us to fly." It was Soren who blurted out the words. The idea half formed seemed to explode at once in his head, sending tremors all the way down to his gizzard. There was a stunned silence. Gylfie and Grimble both looked at Soren and blinked but remained wordless.

"But you know, Soren, and you know, Gylfie, I can tell you what to do, and I can help you practice, but I cannot do everything. It's very strange with flying. A young owl can do everything just perfectly but if you don't believe . . ."

Gylfie and Soren both blinked at Grimble and together said, "If you don't believe, then you'll never fly."

"Yes, yes. I see you understand. And, of course, that is why none of the owlets in the glaucidium will ever fly. It is not only that the vampire bats quiet their stirrings and cause their feathers to turn brittle, but if an owl is moon blinked it, of course, has no notion of what it means to believe."

"But we aren't moon blinked," Gylfie said. "And I don't believe you are either, Grimble."

"You give me hope, you two young ones. I thought all of my hope had been destroyed, but you give me hope. Yes, I shall try. Here is what we must do."

So Grimble explained to them that he was in charge of organizing the products of the pellets — the teeth, the fur, and the flecks — after each day's work. "I store them in the library and keep lists, inventories. I can get you a pass to help in the listings. I work mostly in a small area off the library and then take them in when I get enough. When I don't do that, I am on day guard of the library. You will never be permitted in the library, but I can try to teach you how to fly in that small space. It isn't ideal but it is the only place we have. It connects to the library, which is larger, but you can't go in there because when I am in the inventory area someone else is guarding the library."

"I thought the library had books," Gylfie said.

"It does. But we store these materials there, too. Near the books that supposedly explain them."

"Gylfie feels somehow deep in her gizzard that the flecks might help us escape."

"Don't depend on such things," Grimble said sharply. "Your own belief in yourself will help you much more than any fleck ever will."

And so it was arranged. Gylfie and Soren would be

given passes to help in the inventory area, the inventorium, each night during the newing and on various nights until the moon was full again and all owlets were required in the glaucidium for moon blinking. Their first lesson would begin that very evening.

CHAPTER TWENTY-ONE

To Fly

More flap, deeper flap. Your wings must almost meet on the upstroke of the flap . . ." Grimble directed. Soren and Gylfie were exhausted. This was much harder than anything either one of them had ever seen their parents or older siblings try to do.

"I know you're tired, but the only way out of here is straight up. You have to build your muscles. That's why I am not even having you practice hopping or branching. You do not have the luxury of gliding gently down from a nest. You have to develop your power-flight skills. So try it again."

"But once we're out," Soren asked, "how will we know what to do?"

"You'll know. What did I tell you? The still air has no shape. In the sky you will feel the mass of air as it moves around your wings. You will sense its speed, if it is bumpy or smooth, hot or cold. And you will know how to shape it and use it. Wind always has shape but there is no wind in

St. Aggie's. It is too deep for the wind to reach. And in these small spaces it is hard to even feel the air. It is dead, unmoving air in here. So you must work extra hard to give it a shape with your power strokes, your flapping. Your downstroke is your most powerful. On your upstroke, you want the air to flow through easily. That is why both of you have those feathers with slots, tip slots at the end of your wings. They separate and let you go up easily."

Grimble demonstrated. He pressed forward just a bit, extended his head, and lifted his wings. And that was it — he was suddenly airborne. Twice Soren's size or more, yet Grimble seemed to float up effortlessly. Would they ever learn? Had they even improved?

Grimble almost seemed to read their minds. "This is just your third lesson. You've grown stronger. I can see that. But you must believe it."

And then, by their fourth lesson, it did seem easier and that was the first time they began to perhaps feel the belief in their gizzards. They could feel the air parting above them. They had each flown higher in the deep stone box of the inventorium than they ever had before. They tried to imagine bursting out of it into the welcoming blackness of the moonless night. They could begin to sense the contours of the bubble of air that formed beneath each wing and buoyed them up into the darkness. The newing would last for another two nights and then their learning sessions would begin to dwindle as the moon swelled, and they would be required to stay in the glaucidium for longer and longer exposures to its light for moon blinking. Finally, after the moon had grown fat and full and the first phase of the dwenking began, they would leave. They must leave at that time, for the vampire bats would be returning. It would be their time, as fully fledged owls, to submit to the bats and then there would be no hope of escape.

Although they had not yet been in the library, they would go there on the night of their escape, for, indeed, it was located higher and closer to the sky than any other region aside from the hatchery. Grimble planned to tell the library guard on duty for that night that he would relieve him for a few minutes as a disturbance had been reported in the pelletorium, in the very area that this guard supervised during the day. Grimble promised them that flying would seem easy after all their practice in the deep hole of the inventorium. They were curious about the library. Grimble had tried to explain what it looked like and how the books and the feathers and the teeth, the bones, the flecks, and all the bits that they picked out of the pellets during the day were arranged and stored. It was also in the library that some of the best battle claws were kept. Gylfie and Soren were very curious about them.

"They don't make them here, do they?" Gylfie had asked.

"No. They don't know how. Oh, how they wish they did. I hear Spoorn and Skench talking about it all the time. It requires a deep knowledge of metals, I think. They steal them. They go on raids to various kingdoms where owl chiefs keep fighting owls. They go into fields after battles and collect them from dead warriors. But they don't know how to make them. You see, you think these owls are smart here at St. Aegolius, but Skench and Spoorn are so frightened of any owl being smarter than they are . . . well, that is why they moon blink everyone. No one else really knows how to read here. No questions allowed. So how can anything be learned, be invented? It's impossible. They've been trying to figure out flecks for years, but I doubt they ever will. They never let anyone else study them and maybe find something out. Why, look at you, Gylfie. You, just through wondering and having feelings in your gizzard about flecks, probably know almost as much as they do — because you're curious. But enough talk. Come on you two, time to practice. I want you each to go for that highest chink in the stone wall tonight. Soren, you get five wing beats to do it. Gylfie, since you're smaller, I'll give you eight."

"You have to be kidding," Soren gasped.

"I am not kidding. You're first, Soren. Make every downstroke count. If you believe, you won't ever go yeep."

Soren closed his eyes as he stood on a low stone perch that jutted from the wall. He lifted his wings then, with all his might, powered down. *I can do this! I can do this!* He felt his body lift. He felt the air gather under his wings on the next upstroke. It was a big cushion of air.

"Good!" whispered Grimble. "Again. More powerful." Soren was halfway up the wall to the chink and he had used only two downstrokes.

I can do it, I can do it! I feel the air. I feel the force of my strokes. I am going up. I am going up. I shall fly. . . .

CHAPTER TWENTY-TWO
The Shape of the Wind

Tonight? Grimble, you must be yoicks. It's not anywhere near the dwenking. It's too soon!" Gylfie cried.

"We're not ready," protested Soren.

"You are ready. Soren, I gave you five strokes to get to the chink in the inventorium and you got there in four. Gylfie, I gave you eight and you got there in seven. Tonight is the night."

"Why?" they both said at once.

Grimble sighed. He was going to miss these two. He might miss their questions most of all. It felt so luxurious to be able to ask and answer questions. He had once thought the sweetest taste in the world was that of a freshly killed vole, but now he knew differently. The sweetest thing was a question on the tongue. A word beginning with that wonderful rush of air that w's made. Oh, how he would miss these two young owls. They were lovely to look at, too, in their coats of newly fledged feathers untouched by vampire bats. "The thermals are coming this evening. This is why you must go."

"Thermals? What are thermals?" Soren asked.

"Warm drafts of air. They've arrived earlier than usual. They'll make flying very easy for you once you get out of here. You should meet up with them within a short distance from here. You'll be able to soar."

"We don't know how to soar," Gylfie said. "All we know how to do is flap."

"Don't worry. You'll know exactly what to do when you meet the thermals. The shape of the wind will tell you."

"Who is on guard tonight?"

"It's Jatt."

"Jatt!" Soren gasped. "That's terrible. How will you get him to go to the pelletorium?"

"I'll think of something. Don't worry. I'll get him out of there. I've already got you a pass for tonight between the third and fourth sleep march."

The third sleep march had just finished. Soren and Gylfie sought out the sleep correction monitor in their area and showed them their passes. He blinked and told them to be off. They made their way silently through the stone corridors of St. Aegolius, alone with their thoughts.

Yet those thoughts were the same, for they were deep in concentration as they tried as hard as they ever had to believe in their own ability to fly. They tried not to let themselves be distracted by the fact that the sum total of their flight experience had covered only a very small range of the usual maneuvers a young and newly fledged owl practices. They had no real knowledge of gliding, soaring, or hovering.

"Words, words, words," Grimble would mutter if they ever brought up these notions that they had heard their parents discussing with older siblings. It was Gylfie who mostly asked such questions. And Grimble would always admonish her. "You're thinking too much. You don't need to know anything about hovering and soaring. All you need to know is rapid takeoff straight up — THRUST! POWER FLAPPING!" He poked his head forward as he said each word and fixed Soren and Gylfie in the fierce, uncompromising glare of his yellow eyes. "That's it! That is all you need to get out of here."

So that is what Soren and Gylfie thought of. It filled their minds. The power downstroke. The bunching together of the slots on the leading edge of their primaries. The upstroke, the spacing of those same feathers so the air could pass through with no drag. They had become very muscular from all their practice. They were probably the most muscular young owls in the entire academy of St. Aegolius. This alone should make them believe. Had there ever been an Elf Owl as young as Gylfie who could power flap so strongly?

They arrived at last at the inventorium. Grimble could immediately tell that both owlets were concentrating fiercely. This was good. Now he just hoped that his ruse to get Jatt out would work. Luckily, Grimble had detected that things were not perfect between the two brothers Jutt and Jatt. Perhaps it was jealousy. It seemed as if Skench was paying more attention to Jutt than his brother, particularly on battle flights. There was always a bit of contention after a battle as to the dividing up of the battle claws left on a field from the defeated owls. Skench and Spoorn got first choice and then, when they returned to St. Aggie's, the rest of the claws were sorted and handed out according to rank or battle performance. There was an elderly owl, Tumak, who was the director of the main battle claw repository. But now Grimble was going to tell a bold lie that he hoped would get Jatt out of the library he was guarding. He began talking quite loudly. Soren and Gylfie couldn't imagine what he was doing, for he seemed to be speaking not to them but to some invisible owl.

"You don't say! My word. Trouble in the claw repository. Oh, Jatt's not going to like that at all. I think I better tell him." By the time Grimble, and it was only a matter of seconds, got to the guardhouse of the library, Jatt's feathers were puffed and quivering with agitation. He seemed twice his size and was in obvious pain. If any creature could be swollen with questions it was Jatt. And that, of course, was Grimble's advantage that he planned to work to the fullest.

"Don't worry, Jatt. I shall tell you everything. At least all that I know. Now calm yourself. I had heard Jutt talking with Spoorn earlier, regarding those new battle claws and how he felt Tumak was not handling them correctly. Spoorn had said that she would take it up with Skench."

"Oh, no!" Jatt gasped. "Jutt's been wanting to be the director of the repository forever. And we all know what that means. He'll be the most powerful owl around here next to Skench and Spoorn."

"Well, it is my understanding that they are allowing Tumak and Jutt to fight it out. There's a duel about to begin and Jutt has his forces assembled. Go get your troops, Jatt. Quick — there's still time. I'll stand guard."

"Thank you, Grimble. Thank you. And don't worry. When I am head of the repository, you shall get first choice for battle claws."

"I'm not worried, Jatt. Now, just go while there is still time."

As soon as Jatt turned the corner and disappeared down the long stone crack, Grimble called to Soren and Gylfie. "Come on, you two. There's not a minute to waste." The two owlets raced into the library. They gasped when they entered the room. It was not the books they noticed or the small array of polished battle claws hanging off one wall. It was the sky, black, chinked with stars, stars that seemed so close that an owl could have reached out with a talon and plucked one. Memories rushed back. Memories of sky and breezes — yes, indeed, they did feel a wind, even here. Oh, they were so close. Yes, they believed! Yes, they could do this and, then, just as Soren and Gylfie swung their wings up into their first stroke, Skench burst in. She was ferocious looking in full war regalia. Immense battle claws made her talons twice their size. A metallic needle extended from the tip of her beak and glimmered in the slice of the new moon that hung like a blade over the library.

"Flap!" screeched Grimble. "Flap. You will do it! You will do it! Believe! Power stroke! Power! Two wing beats and you're up." But the two little owls seemed frozen in their fear. Their wings hung like stones at their sides. They were doomed.

Soren and Gylfie watched transfixed as Skench advanced toward them, and then something very peculiar happened. Skench, moved by a power unseen, suddenly slammed into the wall, the wall that had the notches that Grimble had described in which the flecks were stored.

"Go! This is your chance!" Grimble shouted.

An indeed it was. Skench seemed to have been immobilized, paralyzed.

Soren and Gylfie began to pump their wings. They felt themselves rise.

"You can do it! You believe! Feel it in your gizzard. You are a creature of flight. Fly, my children. Fly!" And then there was a terrible shriek and the night was splattered with blood.

"Don't look back! Don't look back, Soren! Believe!" But this time it was not Grimble calling. It was Gylfie. Just as they reached the stone rim, they felt a curl of warm air. And it was as if vast and gentle wings had reached out of the night, and swept them up into the sky. They did not look back. They did not see the torn owl on the library floor. They did not hear Grimble, as he lay dying, chant in the true voice of the Boreal Owl, in tones like chimes in the night, an ancient owl prayer: *"I have redeemed myself by giving belief to the wings of the young. Blessed are those who believe, for indeed they shall fly."*

CHAPTER TWENTY-THREE
Flying Free

In the dark soul of that night, Soren and Gylfie only saw the stars and the moon on its silvery path into the infinite blackness of this new heaven through which they wheeled in flight. So once more the world spiraled. But this time there was a difference. It was Soren who was carving these spirals and loops. With his wings he scooped air, shaped it. There was not the desperate need for flapping and pumping now. Instinctively, he stilled his wings and rode the thermal updrafts, rising higher without even stirring a feather. He looked down at Gylfie, who was a few feet below him, catching the lower layer of the same updraft. Grimble was right. They knew exactly what to do. Instinct and belief flowed through the hollow bones of the two owls as they flew into the night.

It had seemed that after being locked in the still air of the windless canyons and ravines of St. Aegolius, the two owls were encountering every kind of wind and draft imaginable. Soren had not known how long they had flown when he heard Gylfie call out, "Hey, Soren, any idea how we land?"

Land? Landing had been the furthest thing from Soren's mind. He felt as if he could fly forever. But he supposed that the little Elf Owl might be getting tired. For every one stroke of Soren's wings, Gylfie had to make three. "No idea, Gylfie. But maybe we should look for a nice treetop and then . . ." He paused. "Well, I'm sure we'll figure it out."

And they did. Tipping slightly downward at a gentle angle, they began a long glide toward a cluster of trees. Once more, instinct took over as both owls in their descent began to inscribe tighter and tighter circles around the trees below. Each owl angled its wings slightly to increase the drag and then, as they approached the tree, they extended their talons.

"I did it!" Soren gasped as he lighted down on a branch.

"Aiyee!" squeaked Gylfie.

"Gylfie, where are you? What's wrong?"

"Well, except for being upside down, I think I am fine."

"Great Glaux!" Soren exclaimed as he saw the little Elf Owl hanging by her talons with her head pointing toward the ground. "How did that happen?"

"Well, if I knew how, it wouldn't have happened," Gylfie replied testily.

"Oh, dear! What are you going to do?"

"Well, I'm going to think about it."

"Can you do that hanging upside down?"

"Of course I can. What do you think? My brains are going to fall out of my head? Really, Soren!"

Gylfie looked a bit ridiculous hanging upside down, but Soren certainly wasn't going to say anything. He wished he could be of more help.

"If I were you, gal..." A voice came from another branch higher up in the tree.

"Who's that?" Soren was suddenly frightened.

"What does it matter who I am? Been in the same spot as your friend there once or twice myself." Soren felt the branch he was perched on shake. The most enormous owl he had ever seen alighted, then swaggered out toward the end. The owl, a silvery gray color, seemed to simply melt out of the moonlight, but he towered over Soren. His head alone, with his enormous facial disk, was almost twice the size of Gylfie. It was very difficult for Soren to imagine that this huge owl had ever been in the same situation as Gylfie.

"Here's what you have to do," he called down to Gylfie in a deep voice. "You have to let go, just let go! Then quickly flap your wings up, an upstroke, hold it for a count of three. You'll come out right side up and then just glide down. Let me demonstrate."

"But you're so big and Gylfie's so small," Soren said.

"I am big — right you are! But I am delicate and beautiful. I can float! I can skim." The enormous owl had lifted off the branch and was flying through the air, performing every imaginable flourish of flight — plunges, twists, swoops, and loops.

He began a hooting song:

> *Flutter like a hummingbird,*
> *Dive like an eagle,*
> *Ain't no bird that's my equal.*

"Good Glaux!" Soren muttered. "What a show-off."

"Hey, when you got it you show it. When you don't, you usually don't know it." The huge owl lit down, obviously pleased with his wit and flying.

"All right," Gylfie said.

"Letting go is the hardest part, but you got to believe it will work."

Belief again, thought Soren. That seemed to be the word that struck Gylfie as well, because in just that instant Gylfie let go. There was a little blur in the night — like a small leaf caught in a sudden gust — and then Gylfie was flying right side up.

"Beautiful!" exclaimed Soren. In another second, Gylfie had alighted on the branch next to Soren.

"See? Nothing to it," said the huge silvery owl. "'Course I didn't have anyone to coach me. Had to figure it out on my own."

Soren studied the big owl. He seemed young despite his size. He didn't want to be rude but he was genuinely curious about this owl. "Are you from these parts?" Soren asked.

"Here, there, everywhere," the owl replied. "You name it, I've been there." He had a rough manner of speaking that was slightly intimidating.

Gylfie hopped out toward the end of the branch. "I want to thank you for your kindness in advising me on my predicament." Soren blinked. He had never heard Gylfie speak this way. She sounded so much older than she was, and extremely courteous. "We don't mean to be rude but we have never seen an owl of your size. May we be so bold as to inquire as to your species?"

Species! Soren thought. *Where in the name of Glaux did Gylfie come up with these words?*

"Species? What the Glaux is that? Very fancy word for a Great Gray Owl like myself."

"Oh, so you are a Great Gray. I've heard of them, though there were none in Kuneer," Gylfie said.

"Ah, Kuneer! Been there. No, not a good place for Great Grays. As a matter of fact, I can't really tell you where I'm from. See, I was orphaned at a very young age. Plucked up by a St. Aggie's patrol but managed to drop right into an abandoned nest."

"You escaped from a St. Aggie's patrol?"

"You bet. There was no way those idiots were going to take me. Not alive. I bided my time, then bit my snatcher's second talon clean off. He dropped me like a hot coal. They never messed with me again. Word went out, I s'pose." He swaggered a bit, then strutted toward the end of the branch.

Now even Gylfie was speechless. Finally, Soren spoke. "We were snatched as well and only now escaped. I, myself, am from the Kingdom of Tyto, and both Gylfie and I want to find our families again. But we have no idea where we are right now. I mean, that is why I asked who you were. I've never seen your kind in Tyto, but here we are, perched in a Ga'Hoole tree, which are Tyto trees."

"Not necessarily. Ga'Hoole trees follow the River Hoole and the River Hoole runs through many kingdoms."

"Not Kuneer," Gylfie said.

"No, there's not a drop of water in Kuneer, let alone a river."

"Oh, there's water if you know where to look," Gylfie said.

"Hmm." The owl blinked.

Soren could tell right away that this owl was not pleased when someone knew something that he might not.

"So are we in Tyto or not?" Soren asked.

"You're on a border here between Tyto and the Kingdom of Ambala."

"Ambala!" Soren and Gylfie both gasped. Hortense!

"To my way of thinking, it's a second-rate kingdom."

"Second rate!" Soren and Gylfie both said at once.

"Not if you knew Hortense." Soren said.

"Who in the name of Glaux is Hortense?"

"Was," said Gylfie softly.

"A very fine owl," Soren spoke in a tight voice. "A very fine owl indeed."

The huge owl blinked in wonder at these young owls. They seemed to know nothing. And yet ... He let the thought trail off. Certainly their survival skills must be pretty good if they got out of St. Aggie's. Still, there was no education like the one he had received. The education of an orphan. The orphan school of tough learning. He had to learn it all himself. How to fly, where to hunt, what creatures to stalk and which to avoid at all costs. No, nothing could compare to figuring out on one's own the hard rules and schemes of a forest world — a world with uncountable riches and endless perils. It took a tough owl to figure it all out. And that was exactly how Twilight thought of himself. Tough.

Gylfie seemed to have recovered. "Well, permit us to introduce ourselves. I am Gylfie, Elf Owl, more formally know as Micrathene whitneyi, common to desert regions, migratory, cavity nester."

"I know, I know. Spent some time in a hollowed-out cactus with some of you fellows. Hunting skills . . . uh, how should I put it? Well, if all you eat is snake, let's just say desert smarts are different from forest smarts."

"We eat more than snake. My goodness. We eat voles and mice, but not rats — they're a bit large for us."

"Well, never mind." The big owl turned and blinked at Soren. "So what's your story, kid?" Soren had the feeling he should be briefer than Gylfie and not go into so much detail.

"Soren of Tyto, Barn Owl." Soren sensed that going into the rareness of their breed, Tyto alba, would not interest this owl. As a matter of fact, not much impressed this owl. "Lived in an old fir tree with my parents until . . ." His voice dwindled off.

"Until that horrible day." The big owl blinked and tapped Soren lightly with his beak in a gentle preening gesture. This small movement more than anything surprised Soren and Gylfie. The two owls had not seen nor felt the soothing preening gestures since they had fallen from their nests. But preening had been a large part of their lives. Gently prinking with their beaks, the parents would pick out bits and plump up the feathers of their mates and their children as well, or whatever patchy down a baby owl might have sprouted. It was so soothing and lovely. Preening and being preened by one's family and closest of kin and friends was the essence of being a true owl. Soren was overcome by the kindness of the gesture. The big owl turned to Gylfie and spoke. "You, too, little one with the big words, come over here. Bet it's been a while since anyone prinked your down." And so Gylfie hopped over closer to the owl, and while he preened one and then the other in turn, the Great Gray began to tell some of his story.

"My name is Twilight. I don't know how I got the name. It's just my name."

"It fits you," Soren said softly. "Because you are all silvery and gray."

"Yes, not black or white. It fits, and blast my gizzard if I didn't hatch on the edges of time, for that is one of my first memories. Twilight! That silvery border of time between day and night. Most owls have pride in their night vision. We see things that other birds cannot see from high up in the pitch of the night — a mouse, a vole, a tiny squirrel scuttling through the forest. I can see all that, too, but I can also see at a harder time — twilight — when the boundaries become dim and the shapes begin to melt away. I live on the edges and I like it."

"What are you doing here near the edge of Tyto?"

"I have heard that there is a place and that the best way to find it is by following the River Hoole. This stream that flows beneath this Ga'Hoole tree I figure must flow into the River Hoole, or else why would a Ga'Hoole tree grow here?"

Soren and Gylfie both nodded. This seemed to them to be a sensible conclusion. "Is this place," Gylfie asked, "on the edge of something?"

"Actually, it is, I think, more like the middle of something. But I am interested."

"Middle of what?" Soren asked.

"The River Hoole flows into a huge lake. Some call it a sea, Hoolemere, and in the middle of it there is an island. And on the island is a tree. A great tree. It is called the Great Ga'Hoole Tree. It is the greatest of all the Ga'Hoole trees. The most enormous tree that ever grew, some say, and it is the center of a Kingdom called Ga'Hoole."

Soren felt his breath catch in his throat. His eyes widened. He felt Gylfie grow still.

"You mean it's real?" Soren asked.

"It's not just a legend?" Gylfie said, her voice soft with wonder.

"Well, I believe in legends," Twilight said simply. And for the first time all the boastfulness left his voice.

"And what is there, in this great tree that grows on an island in the middle of a sea called Hoolemere?" asked Soren.

"A band of owls, very strong, very brave." Twilight seemed to swell up even bigger before their very eyes as he spoke.

"And," Soren continued, "do these owls rise each night into the blackness and perform noble deeds?" The words of his father flowed through him. "And speak no words but true ones, and their purpose is to right all wrongs, to make strong the weak, mend the broken, vanquish the proud, and make powerless those who abuse the frail? And with hearts sublime, they do take flight. . . . Is this the place of which you speak?"

"Indeed it is," Twilight replied. "All these owls work and fight together, for the good of all kingdoms."

"Do you really believe this place exists?" Soren asked.

"Do you believe you can fly?" Twilight shot back.

Soren and Gylfie both blinked. What a strange answer. It was not an answer at all. It was a question. How far they had come from St. Aegolius Academy for Orphaned Owls!

CHAPTER TWENTY-FOUR
Empty Hollows

"You two are going to have to learn how to hunt. Whatever did they feed you in that place?" Twilight asked.

Soren's and Gylfie's beaks were bloody from tearing at the tender flesh of a vole that Twilight had brought. They had never tasted anything so good. There was an acorn fragrance to this vole, mixed with the withered berries that had dropped from the Ga'Hoole tree in which they still perched. Finally, Gylfie answered, "Mostly crickets, unless you worked in the hatchery."

"That's all?"

"Crickets — day in, day out, every meal."

"Great Glaux, how can an owl live on that — no meat?"

Soren and Gylfie shook their heads, not wanting to miss a bite.

Twilight realized that it would be useless to talk to these two half-starved owls until they were well fed. So when Soren and Gylfie had finished with the vole, he fixed them in the hard glare of his yellow eyes. "So, I want to know — are you two interested in finding the Great Ga'Hoole Tree?"

Soren and Gylfie exchanged nervous glances.

"Well, yes . . ." said Soren.

"And no," said Gylfie.

"Well, which is it? Yes or no?"

"Both," Gylfie said. "Soren and I talked about it when you were off hunting. We would like to go there, of course, but first . . ." Gylfie hesitated.

"But first you want to see if your families are still there."

"Yes," both owls answered meekly. They knew that for Twilight, who had been an orphan almost from the moment he had hatched, it must be hard to understand. He had no memories of nest or family. He had flitted from one place to another, one kingdom to another. He had even lived with creatures not of his own kind — there was a family of woodpeckers in Ambala that had taken him in, an elderly eagle in Tyto, and, most extraordinary of all, a family of desert foxes in Kuneer, which was why Twilight never, ever hunted fox. To eat a fox was unthinkable to Twilight.

"All right. From what you tell me we would not have to go too far out of the way. Our main route follows the river and, Soren, you said your family lived within sight of the river and, well, Gylfie, I know Kuneer very well. I think from what you've told me that your family must have lived by the big gulch."

"Yes, yes! We did."

"That gulch is a dry riverbed that was made by the River Hoole a long, long time ago. So we don't have to go that far off our route."

"Oh, and we promise we'll learn how to hunt. We really will," Soren said.

"Is hunting like flying and . . ." Gylfie offered tentatively, "finding the Great Ga'Hoole Tree — one must believe?"

"Oh, for Glaux's sake, it's only food!" Twilight said with mild disdain.

The three owls left at first black. It had turned quite cold. No thermals to ride, and both Soren and Gylfie realized how lucky they had been — or rather how smart Grimble had been to insist on their leaving at the time of the unseasonable drafts of warm air. It was a lot easier flying on those rising thermals. There were none on this bright winter night but still it was lovely to be free, and the world below, keen with frost, sparkled fiercely. Oh, how Soren wished his parents could see him fly. He flapped his wings, increased his forward thrust, and sailed higher into the sky. "The Yonder! The Yonder!" as Mrs. Plithiver called the sky. Dear Mrs. P. He missed her, too. Oh, he could tell her about the Yonder now. He could tell that dear old blind snake all about the Yonder himself.

By the next day, it had begun to snow very hard. At times, the snow was a blinding fury. Soren's transparent eyelids swept back and forth almost constantly to clear off the snowy crystals. Sometimes the snow was so thick that the sky and the earth below seemed to blend into one mass of grayness. There were no edges. The horizon had melted into nothingness and it was through this blurry world that Twilight navigated with unbelievable skill and grace. They followed him closely, Soren flying on his upwind or weather wing, with Gylfie on the other side in the lee of Twilight's downwind wing.

"You see, you two, the world is not always black and white — what did I tell you?" Twilight spoke as he expertly guided them through the thickening snow flurries.

"How do you do it?" Soren asked.

"I learned the hard edges of things in the daylight and the night, but then I learned how this is not the only way of seeing. That, in fact, other things might be hidden when it seems the clearest. So I unlearned some things."

"How do you unlearn something?" Soren asked.

"You decide not to trust only in what you can see. You

look for a new way and clear your mind of the old way. You try to feel new things in your gizzard."

"Sounds hard," Gylfie said.

"It is. Oh! All right, enough talk. Prepare to glide. Remember, Gylfie, what I told you about sticking out your talons. We don't want you upside down again."

"Yes, Twilight, I'll remember. Talon extension is vitally important."

"Little owl, big words," Twilight muttered to himself.

"Well, maybe I was wrong. Maybe it wasn't so close to the river. Maybe it wasn't a fir tree after all."

Twilight and Gylfie looked at each other. This was the third tree that they had visited. There was not a sign of an owl family living in any of the trees, but in two of the three, this last one included, there were hollows and definite signs of owls having once nested in them. "You know my memory isn't really perfect," Soren said weakly. "I . . . I . . . could have —"

Gylfie interrupted. "Soren, I think they've gone."

Soren turned on the little Elf Owl. "How can you say that, Gylfie? How can you ever say that?" Soren was trembling with rage. "You don't know them. I know them. My parents wouldn't have left — ever."

"They didn't leave you, Soren," Gylfie said in a very

small voice. "They thought that you were gone forever, snatched."

"No! No! They would believe! They would believe like the way we were taught to believe in flying. They would believe, and my mother would never agree to leave this place. She would always hope that I would come back."

And it was when Soren said the word "hope" that something deep inside him collapsed. It almost felt as if his gizzard was shriveling up. He began to weep with the unthinkable notion of his parents giving up hope for him. Shudders racked his entire body. His feathers, stiff with frost, quivered.

Then Twilight spoke, "Soren, they're gone. Maybe something happened to them. You shouldn't take it personally. Buck up now, old buddy."

"Personally? What do you know, Twilight, that is personal about any family? You've never had a family. Remember, you're always telling us about how much you learned in your own orphan school of tough learning. You don't know the feel of a mother's down. You don't know what it's like to hear stories from a father, or to hear him sing. Do you know what a psalm is, Twilight? I bet you don't. Well, we Barn Owls know about psalms and books and the feeling of down."

Twilight's feathers had ruffled up, spiky with ice crystals. He looked fearsome. "I'll tell you what I know, you miserable little owl. The whole world is my family. I know the softness of a fox's fur, and the strange green light that comes into their eyes during the spring moons. I know how to fish because I learned from an eagle. And when meat is scarce I know how to find the ripest part of a rotten tree and peck the juiciest bugs from it. I know plenty."

"STOP FIGHTING!" Gylfie screamed. "Soren, you're broken, you're sad. I will be the same way."

Soren looked up, startled. "What do you mean 'will be'?"

"What do you think the chances are of my family being found?" She didn't wait for Soren to answer the question. "I'll tell you. None."

"Why?" Soren said. Even Twilight seemed surprised. "We were snatched, Soren. Do you think any owl parents would stay in the same place? Those St. Aggie's patrols know where to find owls. They'd come back. They'd look for young owl chicks. Any family with any sense would move on. They wouldn't want to lose all their chicks. And I think I know where mine would go."

"Where?" Soren asked.

"The Great Ga'Hoole Tree," Gylfie spoke quietly.

"Why?" Soren blinked. "You're not even sure it's a real place. What did you call it?"

"Tales of Yore."

"Yes, Tales of Yore. Why, in the name of Glaux, would your family take off for a Yore place, not proven, not real?"

"Because maybe they were desperate," Gylfie said.

"That's no reason."

Then Gylfie answered in a stronger voice, "Because they felt it in their gizzards."

"How do you feel a legend in your gizzard? You're talking racdrops, Gylfie." It made Soren feel good to use a bad word. But at the same time he felt he was betraying his own father. For hadn't his father said that one began to feel a legend in one's gizzard and over time it could become true in one's heart? "Racdrops!" he repeated. "Complete nonsense, Gylfie, and you know it." As angry as Soren was, what he had just uttered made him feel worse.

"Since when has anything made sense? Does St. Aggie's make sense? Do Skench and Spoorn make sense?"

"Grimble made sense," Soren said in barely a whisper.

"Yes," Gylfie replied, and reached out with the tip of her wings to touch Soren.

Twilight had remained quiet. Finally, he spoke. "I am going to search for the Great Ga'Hoole Tree. You two are welcome to join me. Gylfie, it is not far out of our way to go by the Desert of Kuneer. Even though I think you're right about your parents, maybe for your own peace of mind you should make sure. We can start for there tonight."

"Yes, I suppose you're right."

"You'll never be at peace if you don't know for sure," Twilight added.

At peace? Soren thought. *Am I at peace now?* And it was as if a tiny sliver of ice had burrowed into his gizzard, for Soren knew only one thing for sure, which was that the two owls who had loved him most in all the world were gone, gone far away, and he was far from feeling peaceful.

They would sleep for the rest of this day and begin their desert flight at night. Nights were the best for desert flights, Twilight said, especially in the time of the dwenking. Soren was too tired to ask why. Too tired to hear some long explanation of Twilight's. Twilight seemed to know an awful lot and liked talking about it, always weaving in some story of a narrow escape or something that pointed up his extreme cleverness. But Soren was simply too tired to listen this morning. "Good light," he said in a small voice.

"Good light, Soren," Gylfie said.

"Good light, Soren and Gylfie," Twilight said.

"Good light, Twilight," Soren and Gylfie both said together.

Soren was soon asleep in the hollow. It felt good to sleep in a hollow, even if it was an empty one, with his head tucked under his wing in a normal sleeping position.

Then a voice, a familiar voice, pierced his sleep. He felt himself frozen and unable to move. It was as if he had gone yeep, his wings locked. Was he dreaming or sleeping? It was Grimble's voice. They were back in the library of St. Aggie's. Soren was madly pumping his wings. "Go! This is your chance," the voice cried. And then a terrible shriek. "Don't look back. Don't look back." But they did.

"Wake up, wake up! You two are both having terrible dreams. Wake up." It was Twilight shaking them. Soren and Gylfie awoke together with the same terrible image of a torn owl, bleeding and mortally wounded.

"It's Grimble," Gylfie said. "He's dead."

"I know. We both dreamed the same dream but . . . but . . . but, Gylfie, it was just a dream. Grimble might be fine."

"No," Gylfie said slowly. "No. I tried not to look but I caught a glimpse. The torn wings, his head at a weird angle." Gylfie's voice dwindled into the first dim gray of the coming night.

"Why didn't you say anything?"

"Because," she hesitated. It sounded so stupid, but it

was the truth. "Because I was flying. I had just felt that first soft cushion of air beneath my wings. I was about to soar and I forgot everything. I was just wings . . . and . . ."

Soren understood. It was not stupid. It was just the way they were. In the moment Grimble had died, they had become what they were always intended to be. Their destiny had been rendered. Flight was theirs.

"Well, buck up, you two," Twilight said gruffly. "I want to leave at first black. That will be in minutes. So it should be a perfect night for flying to Kuneer. And let me tell you, there is nothing, simply nothing, like desert flying. And you two can get in some hunting practice. Nice juicy snakes they have in Kuneer."

"I don't eat snakes," Soren said tersely.

"Oh, racdrops!" Twilight muttered under his breath. This owl was finicky. He mustered all the patience he could. "You don't eat snakes? Kindly explain."

"Well," said Gylfie. "You don't eat foxes."

Twilight blinked. "It's an entirely different situation. Few owls do eat foxes anyway. But snakes — snakes are a basic owl food. Look, I can't handle this kind of stuff. Are you stark-raving yoicks? Don't eat snakes. When I was your age I ate anything. Anything to keep me alive and flying. What do you mean you don't eat snakes? What owl doesn't eat snakes?"

"He doesn't," Gylfie said calmly. "It's a family thing. They had an old nest-maid who was a snake, a kind of nursemaid, as well, for the young ones, so it's out of respect for her, Mrs. Plithiver." Soren was touched that Gylfie remembered Mrs. Plithiver's name.

"And as much as I would love to see Mrs. Plithiver, I surely hope she does not hear our conversation," Soren added.

Twilight blinked and shook his head in an exaggerated manner and muttered something about coddled owls and the orphan school of tough learning. "Nest-maids? Nursemaids?" His head seemed to spin around entirely on his neck as he walked out to the end of the branch, muttering to himself and punching the air with his talons in frustration. "Unbelievable! Bless my sweet gizzard. Next thing they'll be telling me is that they had another owl to do the family flying for them and hunt as well. I tell you, I wouldn't give a pile of racdrops for such a life."

CHAPTER TWENTY-FIVE

Mrs. P.!

They were on a border of scrub between the forest they had left behind and the desert that glimmered ahead in the distance. Twilight said they should take a rest and Soren, still irritated with Twilight's muttering about his and Gylfie's "coddled" upbringing, was determined now to prove himself as a hunter. So while Twilight and Gylfie tucked their heads under their wings for a quick nap, Soren flew off to find a vole or a mouse or perhaps even a rat.

It was not, however, the heartbeat of a mouse that Soren heard, for it was much too slow, but it was a heartbeat. And between two beats did he hear something else as well? A soft whispering sound full of strange agony. Very few creatures have ever heard a snake weep. There are no tears but they weep nonetheless, and that is how Soren found Mrs. Plithiver. He alighted on an old moss-covered stump. There, nestled at the bottom of the stump where two roots poked up, he saw a pale coil glimmering in the light of the nearly full moon. He tipped his head over the edge.

"Mrs. P.?" Soren blinked. He was incredulous.

A tiny head lifted out of the coiled body. There were the two dents where eyes might have been. "Mrs. P.," Soren said again.

"Mercy! It can't be."

"Mrs. P. It's me, Soren."

"Of course it is! Dear boy! Even an old blind snake like me would know that."

This was incredible. She recognized him. All his worst waking dreams vanished. Mrs. P. uncoiled and began to crawl up the stump.

Oh, it was a joyous reunion. They touched each others' faces gently, and had Mrs. P. possessed eyes, they would have shed tears of joy, but she insisted on slipping, slithering, and slinking her way across and over and under Soren's wings. "Be patient, dear. I want to get a sense of your plumage. Oh, my, you have fledged out beautifully. I bet you fly magnificently."

"But Mrs. P., where are Mum and Da and Eglantine and Kludd?"

"Don't mention that owl's name."

"My brother?"

"Yes, dear. He's the one who shoved you from the nest. I knew he was no good from the minute he hatched."

"But you couldn't see him shove me. How did you know?"

"I sensed it. We blind snakes can sense a lot. I knew you weren't on the rim of the hollow. You would have to be right on the rim to really fall out. You were just looking over the edge. You see, when he shoved you, I had been taking a snooze very close to Kludd's talons. I felt him stir. I felt the talons raise up and, well, sort of lurch. And then, of course, did he want me to go get help? No. He tried to stop me, blocked up my exit hole, but I found another all the same. Still, by the time I got back you had been snatched."

Soren closed his eyes and remembered. It all came back. The awful moment. "You're right," Soren said quietly. "You're absolutely right. I was shoved."

"Yes, and I sensed he might do the same to Eglantine. Your parents came back, of course, and they were devastated to find you gone. They gave Kludd strict instructions to mind Eglantine the next time they went hunting. But I knew what was coming. I was frantic when they went on another hunting expedition. I thought I'd have to get help. My friend Hilda worked for some Grass Owls in a tree in

189

another part of the forest. They're a lovely family. I thought maybe they would give me some help. So I sneaked off when Kludd was asleep. Sound asleep, I thought. Well, do you know that by the time I came back Eglantine was gone as well."

"Gone? Where? What did he say?"

"Oh, it makes me tremble to even think of it. He said, 'You breathe a word of this, P., and you'll get what's coming to you.' Well, I couldn't imagine what he thought that was. So I said, 'Young fellow, that is no way to talk to your elders even though I am a servant.' And then . . . oh, this is the hardest . . . he screeched, 'You know, P., I've suddenly developed a taste for snake,' and he swooped down on me."

"Good Glaux!"

"Oh, don't swear, dear boy. It doesn't become one of your station."

"Mrs. P., what did you do?"

"I went down a hole. I waited as long as I could for your parents to return, but I didn't hear anything except that awful Kludd. Well, there was a back way out of this hole and I thought if I wanted to survive I'd better leave. Imagine — I couldn't even give notice to your parents. After all these years, not even to give notice. It really is not a proper way to depart."

"I don't think you had much choice, Mrs. P."

"No, I suppose I didn't."

"Come with me. I've made some friends. We are on our way to Hoolemere."

"Hoolemere!" There was a hiss of excitement in Mrs. Plithiver's small voice.

"You've heard of it and the Great Ga'Hoole Tree?"

"Oh, yes, my dear. It is just this side of Yonder!"

Soren blinked. He felt a wonderful quiver in his gizzard.

"She is NOT for dinner!" Soren glared at Twilight. He had just lit down on the branch that led into the hollow. Mrs. Plithiver was nestled in the feathers just behind his head and between his shoulders. "I want to make that perfectly clear. This is my dear friend, Mrs. Plithiver."

"Mrs. Plithiver!" Gylfie hopped forward on a branch. "*The* Mrs. Plithiver? I am honored. Permit me to introduce myself. I am Gylfie."

"Oh, a little Elf Owl, I believe." Mrs. Plithiver coiled up and raised her head in a greeting. It wavered slightly above Gylfie's head and she could sense her diminutive size. "I am enchanted. Oh, my goodness, you're almost as small as me." Mrs. Plithiver giggled a bit. Laughter in snakes has a slight hiccuppy sound.

"And this is Twilight," Soren said.

"Charmed," Mrs. Plithiver said.

"Likewise," replied Twilight. "Not used to servants, ma'am. Grew up on my own, more or less. Orphan school of tough learning. Not as polished as these two."

"Oh, good manners cannot really be learned, young'un. They are bred."

Twilight looked confused and stepped back a bit.

"Mrs. P., don't worry," Soren said. "I have explained to everyone how I come from a non-snake-eating family, and I expect this rule to be followed." Twilight and Gylfie nodded solemnly.

"Oh, good. I am sure we shall all get along fine."

"Mrs. P. wants to go with us. She can ride between my shoulders."

"I don't know what I'll do for references, of course, if I can find another position," Mrs. P. worried.

"What about me?" Soren said.

"Well, yes, I suppose they'll take the word of a youngster, even though I was actually with your family for much longer than you were. Alas!" She sighed deeply.

"Don't go getting emotional on us, ma'am. We got flying to do." Twilight spoke firmly but not unkindly.

"Of course, I'm so sorry." Mrs. P. gave a little shiver that coursed up her body as if she were trying to shake all such bleak thoughts away. It was almost as if she were shedding her skin.

Then Twilight, perhaps feeling he had been too abrupt with her, added, "I can take you for a spell myself, Mrs. P. I'm bigger than you, Soren. She won't add much weight."

"Oh, aren't you both dear," Mrs. P. said.

"I'm afraid I can't offer any such service," said Gylfie. "I don't think I weigh much more than Mrs. Plithiver. Although I would welcome her charming conversation."

"Oh, how sweet. And I have heard that Elf Owls are wonderful conversationalists." Twilight blinked and muttered something about little owls and big words. "But quite frankly, dear, serving snakes are not encouraged to engage in idle conversation with owls of your station."

"Mrs. P.," Soren said, stepping forward. "Please stop all that."

"All what, dear boy?"

"All this stuff about serving and stations. We are all the same now. There are no stations, no nests, no hollows. We're all orphans. We've all seen horrible things. The world is different now. And part of that difference is that there is no difference between any of us."

"Oh, no, dear boy. There shall always be servants. Don't say that. I come from a long tradition of service. It is nothing to be ashamed of. It is a most noble calling." Soren realized it would be useless to argue with her.

And so the little band of owls, with the blind snake

perched between Soren's shoulders, lifted into flight. The moon still rode high, although a halo of mist seemed to surround it.

"Oh, this is glorious, Soren. I am in the Yonder. Who would have believed it? Oh, my goodness, you are a magnificent flier." Mrs. Plithiver's small voice rang out in sheer ecstasy.

"Hang on, Mrs. P., I have to make a banking turn." Soren really didn't need to make such a turn, but he wanted to show Mrs. P. how gently he could carve the night sky with his wing and angle himself in a new direction. He soon made another one so that he could fall back in with the group.

"Oh, Yonder! Yonder!" Mrs. P. exclaimed again and again. "I am in the Yonder!" Her joy whipped out through the night with a singing hiss that to Soren made the stars shimmer even brighter.

Twilight was right. There was nothing like desert flying. The night was not really black but a deep, dark blue. The sky, moonless, tingled with stars. And although the air was chilly, from time to time heat from the desert sands below rolled up in great waves into the night, turning rough air smooth. The three owls would soar for endless minutes on the soft desert drafts, angling their tail feathers and primaries, carving great arcs in the darkness of the blue, inscribing imaginary figures with their wing tips or perhaps tracing the starry pictures of the constellations.

Twilight did know a lot. He told them the names of the constellations — the Great Glaux, whose one wing pointed toward a star that never moved. There was another one called the Little Raccoon, and then on summer nights, he said, the Big Raccoon rose in the sky and appeared to be dancing, so some called it the Dancing Raccoon. Still another was called the Great Crow because it spread its wings in the early autumn skies. But on this night, they flew under the bright and starry wings of the Great Glaux.

For the first time, Soren realized that his body had really changed. He was a fully fledged owl. It was the utter quiet with which he flew that first made him aware of this change. The last of his plummels had finally sprouted. These soft, fine feathers lay over the surface of his flight feathers, silencing them as he flew.

"I think we're getting near," Gylfie said.

The three owls began a long glide downward. They were now skimming above the sand, just a bit higher than the prickly cactuses. "Don't worry," Gylfie said. "The needles don't hurt. We're too light."

Gylfie had landed and so had Twilight. But just before landing, Soren heard something — a rapid beating sound.

It was a heartbeat. And not that of a snake. In his gizzard Soren knew what it was, a mouse, and his mouth began to water. "Hang on, Mrs. P.! Going in for mouse!"

"Oh, goody!" she cried, and coiled herself tighter into the deep ruff of feathers between his shoulders.

Soren quickly flapped his wings in a series of powerful upstrokes and gained some height. He cocked his head one way, then the other. The heartbeat seemed to pulse across his face. He knew where this creature was and, without even thinking, began a rapid downward spiral.

Within a second, he had the mouse in his talons and had sunk his beak in, just as he had seen his father do when he killed a mouse at the base of their fir tree.

"Good work." Twilight drifted down beside him. "No one can beat you Barn Owls for picking up a mouse's heartbeat." This was the first compliment that Twilight had ever given him.

"Even for one not brought up in the orphan school of tough learning?"

"Not very gracious, Soren!" Mrs. P. hissed softly in his ear. Soren immediately regretted what he had said. "Manners, child!"

"Sorry, Twilight, that wasn't very gracious of me. Thank you for the compliment."

"Gracious!" a voice squeaked. "You call that gracious?

And I'll thank you to take your disgusting talons out of my home."

Soren stepped back and pulled his talons, which were now clutching the mouse, from the sand. From a hole near the base of the cactus from which he had just stepped back, a small face emerged. It was a face not unlike Gylfie's but larger, with brownish feathers and big yellow eyes with a swag of short white feathers above them.

"What in the name of Glaux . . . ?" Soren began to whisper.

"This is wrong. ALL wrong . . ." Twilight gasped.

"Speotyto cunicularia!" Gylfie whispered, then added, "very rare."

"Oh, for Glaux's sake, you and your big words," rasped Twilight.

But at that same moment, there was a terrible shriek and the owl-like thing that had emerged from the hole shrunk back. Then they heard a soft exhalation of air. Twilight stepped up to the hole and peered down. "I think it's fainted."

"What is IT?" Soren asked, completely forgetting the succulent mouse he still clasped in his talons.

"A Burrowing Owl," Gylfie said. "Very rare. But I remember my parents talking about it. It nests in the old burrows of ground animals."

"Oh, Glaux!" both Twilight and Soren said at once, and made gagging noises.

"They don't!" Twilight said, his voice drenched in disbelief. "Well, learn something new every day, even me . . . well, more like every other day. Met an owl who won't eat snakes — oh, pardon me, Mrs. Plithiver."

"No need to apologize," she said quickly. "Soren's family was exceptional in that way. Such elegance they had!" she said wistfully.

"Anyhow, as I was saying," Twilight continued, "then another who lives in holes — not trees. What's the world coming to?"

"I don't think not eating snakes and living in holes of ground animals are quite the same thing. Besides, you said you lived with foxes," Soren said huffily.

"Above foxes, not in their den. Lived in an old cactus hollow. Their den was beneath it."

A rustling noise came from the hole. The three owls stepped a bit closer. A beak poked out. "Is he still there?"

"Who?" asked Gylfie. "We're all still here."

"The one with the white face. The ghost owl."

Twilight and Gylfie spun their heads toward Soren. "Me?"

That was when Soren realized that he had not only fledged the rest of his flight feathers but his face feathers as well. Like all Barn Owls, his face had turned pure white and was rimmed with tan feathers. His belly and the underneath parts of his wings were the same pure white, while the top of his wings, his back, and his head were a mixture of tans and browns delicately speckled with darker feathers. And unlike almost any other owls, his eyes had not turned yellow but were deepest black, which made his face seem even whiter.

"I'm not a ghost," Soren spoke. "I'm a Barn Owl. We all have white faces." Soren felt a strange mixture of pride and terrible sadness. He wished his parents could see him now. He must look a lot like his father. And Eglantine — what would she look like? If she resembled her mother, her face would be white but with a more distinct and darker rim, particularly on the lower part. She might have a few more speckles and they would be darker. She would almost be ready to fly.

"Are you sure?" The owl was creeping a bit farther out of the hole.

"Am I sure what?"

"Are you sure you're not a ghost?"

"Why would I want to pretend to be a ghost? Are you sure you live in that hole?" Soren replied.

"Of course I do. We've always lived in holes. My parents, my grandparents, my great-grandparents, my great-

great-grandparents. And what's with the snake on your head and all this talk about not eating snakes?"

"This is Mrs. Plithiver. She has been with my family a very long time. And," Soren paused dramatically, "we don't eat snake. We not only find it unappetizing but wrong, and my friends here have agreed — not to touch snake. I want to make that perfectly clear. Or you'll be a ghost before you know it!" Soren said, raising his voice.

"Perfectly clear," the Burrowing Owl answered in a quavery voice, and dipped his head toward Mrs. Plithiver. "Pleased to eat ya. I mean, meet ya."

Soren gave a long rasping sound.

"I'm sure it was just a slip of the tongue, Soren," Mrs. P. said diplomatically.

"So what happened to your parents?" Twilight asked abruptly.

The Burrowing Owl hesitated and then sighed. "I don't like to speak about it."

"Were you snatched?"

Again there was a long silence. And then finally the story spilled out in jagged chunks between gasps and sobs. Soren listened. At one point he heard Twilight mutter, "This is one hysterical owl." Gylfie told him to shut up.

The Burrowing Owl was named Digger and he had not been snatched, but his two brothers had been. From the description of the owls who did the snatching, it must have been Jatt and Jutt. The most horrific part of the story, however, was the fight that Jatt and Jutt had over the youngest, Digger's brother Flick. "He was plump, a chubby little fellow, and they . . . they . . . they ate him!"

Digger crumpled into the sand in a swoon. "Come on, now," Twilight said briskly, and nudged the poor owl. "You can't keep passing out. Buck up."

Gylfie and Soren looked at each other in disbelief. Soren thought if he heard Twilight say "buck up" one more time, he might just attack. But it was Gylfie who bristled up and suddenly seemed twice her normal size. "His brother's been eaten by another owl and you say 'buck up'? Twilight, for Glaux's sake, show some sensitivity."

"Sensitivity gets you nowhere in the desert. If he keeps passing out like this, why, if the moon was full, he'd get moon blinked in no time."

A shudder passed through Gylfie and Soren at the mere mention of those words. Digger began to stir. He dragged himself to his feet.

"How did you get away?" Soren asked.

"I ran."

"Ran?" Soren and Twilight both spoke at once. This, indeed, was a very strange owl.

"Well, I hadn't really learned how to fly yet, but we

Burrowing Owls are good at running." Soren looked at Digger's legs. Unlike most owls, Digger's legs barely had any feathers and were exceedingly long. "I ran as far and as fast as I could. You see, our parents were out hunting when all this happened, and these two owls were in such a tussle over Flick. Cunny, the next oldest brother, had already been snatched, and this other owl had flown off with him, although he kept yelling back to the other two not to eat Flick. His voice was odd, softer than the other two owls, a kind of *tingg-tingg* sound. I never heard anything like it."

"Grimble," Soren and Gylfie said at once.

"So what happened?" Twilight asked. "Did your parents come back and find you?"

"Well, the problem is that I'm lost. I ran farther and faster than I ever thought I could and I have been trying to find my way back ever since. Once I came to a burrow that looked just like the one that I had lived in with my parents, but there was no sign of them. So it must have been the wrong burrow." Digger said this in a quavering voice and then added, "Mustn't it?"

Soren, Gylfie, and Twilight remained silent.

"I mean," Digger continued, "they would never just leave. They would think something had happened and they would go out and search for us. One of them would search and the other would stay behind. You know, in case we returned or . . ." His voice died away and was swallowed in the cool breeze of the desert night.

Deep in his gizzard, Soren felt the Burrowing Owl's anguish. "Digger," he said, "they might have come back and seen the . . . the" — he took a deep breath — "the blood and the feathers of your brother on the ground. They might have thought that you had all been murdered. They didn't really leave you, Digger. They probably thought you were all dead."

"Oh," Digger said quietly. And then, "How awful. My parents think I am dead! We all are dead! How terrible. I must find them, then. I must show them that I am alive. I am their son. Why, I can even fly now." But instead of flying he began to stride off with great purpose into the desert.

"Well, why aren't you flying?" Twilight called after him.

Digger spun his head around. "Oh, there's a burrow right over here. I just want to take a look."

"Oh, great Glaux," sighed Gylfie. "He's going to walk all the way across this desert, poking into every burrow."

CHAPTER TWENTY-SIX

Desert Battle

They flew for another night, skirting the edges of the Desert of Kuneer. Nowhere had they found any signs of Gylfie's family, not even in the old cactus where they had all lived together before the snatching.

As they flew, Soren began to think deeply about St. Aggie's and the absolute evilness of the owls there. The evil seemed to have touched almost every kingdom — egg snatching in Ambala, chick snatching in Tyto, and now the worst horror of all, cannabalism in Kuneer. Hortense had told them that a few of the owls in Ambala had somehow figured out that the source of the evil was St. Aggie's, but his own parents had just thought it was something random, perhaps a small gang of renegade owls — nothing as large and powerful as St. Aggie's. They never could have imagined such a place, and Soren felt that few owls in any of the kingdoms could have, either. Was it possible that Soren, Gylfie, and Twilight were the only ones who were aware of the scope and power of St. Aggie's? Were they the only ones who had all the pieces to this horrible puzzle of violence and destruction that was touching every single owl kingdom? If this was true, they must stick together. There was strength in numbers even if the number was only three. They were the three who knew the terrible truth of St. Aggie's. This knowledge alone could help them save other owls.

Soren remembered when he was still a prisoner of St. Aggie's and first realized that it was not simply enough to escape. How awful it had been to imagine his beloved sister, Eglantine, a victim of the brutality of St. Aggie's. He remembered thinking that there was a world of Eglantines out there. So now they had escaped, and now he knew for certain that their task was greater than he and Gylfie and Twilight had ever imagined. Soren knew he must think carefully about how he could explain all this to Twilight and Gylfie.

Every now and then, the three owls would look down and spot Digger trudging through the desert sand. Occasionally, Digger would lift into flight but always skimmed low, combing the desert for any burrow that might shelter his parents. Mostly, however, he would run, his long, nearly featherless legs striking out across the sand, his short stubby tail lifted to catch any wind from behind that would give a boost to his speed. Or if there was a head wind, as now, he would lean into it, tucking his wings close to his body, and ram ahead.

"That fool owl has the strongest legs I've ever seen," Twilight muttered as the first slice of the moon rose in the sky.

"Strongest legs and the stubbornest head," Gylfie added.

But deep within Soren there was a flicker of bright admiration for this odd owl. One had to marvel at Digger's determination. Just as Soren was pondering this, he heard something. He cocked his head one way, then the other.

As in all Barn Owls, Soren's ear openings on either side of his face were not evenly placed — the left one being higher than the right. His uneven set of ears actually helped him to capture sound better. And now he instinctively worked certain muscles in his facial disk to expand its surface and help guide the sounds to his ear. The noise was coming from his windward side, his right ear, because it was that ear that was picking it up before his left ear. Now the sound was arriving almost at the same time in both ears, perhaps with one-millionth of a second difference.

"Triangulating, are you?" Twilight asked.

"What?" Soren said.

"Fancy word for what you Barn Owls do best. Figure out exactly where a sound is coming from. Something tasty down there? I could use a bite."

"Well, there's something below but it's not on the ground. It's off to windward. You can line it up with that bright star on my wing tip."

Then, suddenly, Soren and Gylfie saw them. "Great Glaux, it's Jatt and Jutt!" Soren exclaimed.

"Look!" said Gylfie. "They're closing in on Digger. I hope there's a burrow nearby."

"47-2 is with them," Soren said. "Look at that stupid owl. It's huge now."

"It's a Screech Owl," whispered Twilight. It certainly was, and 47-2 now resembled that other terrible Screech Owl — Spoorn.

"They must have let her grow flight feathers and taught her to fly," Gylfie said weakly.

"Sheer off to downwind," Twilight ordered. "We don't want them to hear us."

"Right, but hush!" said Soren. "I'm picking up something. Let me listen."

The words that Soren picked up from the three owls that flew below them were chilling, even though the conversation broke up on the rising wind currents.

"47-2, once you taste a Burrowing Owl — well ... nothing ... like it ... run fast ... no burrows here ... no place ... hide ..."

"We've got to do something," Soren said.

"The three of them against the two and a half of us." Twilight sighed as he turned his head toward Gylfie.

"I can be a diversion," said Gylfie quickly. And giving the other two owls no time to reply, she plunged into a quick downward spiral.

"What's she doing?" Soren asked. Gylfie was already on the ground and she was doing the best imitation imaginable of a burrowing owl, kicking out her feet as she tried to run across the desert sand.

"Look, it's working!" cried Twilight. And sure enough, 47-2 was turning toward Gylfie.

"Charge!" roared Twilight.

"Hang on Mrs. P.," Soren gasped.

Jatt and Jutt were just lighting down on the sand when Twilight and Soren struck. Soren, his feet forward, spread his talons and thrust his legs straight out. He shut his eyes but felt his talons sink into the feathers between Jatt's ear tufts and then one talon hit something not like feathers at all. It was flesh, then bone. A terrible cry ripped through the night. But now Soren was tumbling in the sand. There was a whirlwind of feathers and dust. Something slithered nearby. He hoped it was Mrs. P. finding herself a safe hole.

Then there was a deep hoot that reverberated across the vastness of the desert. It was Twilight beginning his battle cry. Jatt and Jutt, however, had their own fierce thrum that seemed to shake Soren to his gizzard. Twilight was hooting as only Twilight could.

> *You ugly rat-faced birds.*
> *You call yourself a bird?*
> *You call yourself an owl?*
> *You ain't no decent kind of fowl!*
> *They call you Jatt?*
> *They call you Jutt?*
> *I'm gonna toss you in a rut!*
> *Then I'm gonna punch you in the gut!*
> *Then you're gonna wind up on your butt!*
> *Think you're all gizzard!*
> *I seen better lizards.*
> *One-two-three-four,*
> *You're goin' down, won't ask for more.*
> *Five-six-seven-eight,*
> *You ain't better than fish bait . . .*
> *Nine-ten-eleven-twelve,*
> *I'm gonna send you straight to hell.*

The air was laced with Twilight's taunts. From the corner of his eye, Soren saw Jutt trying to jab at Twilight. But Twilight was as fast as his smart-talking beak. He dodged, he feinted with his jabs, seeming to aim for one place, then stabbing at another, and all the while yammering away in his hooting singsong taunts. First at Jatt, then Jutt. He would lure them in close for a strike and then strike back faster. His talons became a blur. Soren had never seen anything as fast and as light as the immense Great Gray Owl.

Soren tried to keep his focus on closing in on 47-2 before, indeed, she caught up with Gylfie. Suddenly, however, Soren felt something strike him from behind. He flipped in the air and came down on his back. Jatt, much bigger, loomed like a monster owl above him. One ear tuft had been torn off completely. The owl was in a mad frenzy. "I'll kill you! Kill you! I'll rip out your eyes!"

Just as the sharp beak began to come toward him, Soren felt the air stir and a shadow slide across them. Then, miraculously, the huge weight that had pinned him down lifted. Still lying on his back, he blinked in utter amazement as he saw the owl rise above him — not in free flight but in the talons of the most immense bird he had ever seen. Its white head glistened in the light cast from the crescent moon that was now directly overhead.

On the ground to the left, another bird, also with a white head, stalked about the lifeless forms of Jutt and 47-2.

Then Gylfie and Digger walked up. "I've never seen anything like it," Digger said. "Who are they? Who are these white-headed birds?"

"Eagles," Twilight spoke softly with great reverence. "Bald eagles."

"Hortense's eagles!" Soren and Gylfie both said at once.

"Hortense?" said Mrs. Plithiver as she crawled out of her hole. "Who's Hortense?"

CHAPTER TWENTY-SEVEN

Hortense's Eagles

"My name is Streak," said the smaller eagle, "and this is my mate, Zan. She is mute and cannot speak." Zan nodded to the four owls and dipped her beak almost to the desert floor. "Her tongue," Streak continued, "was torn out by the evil ones."

"The evil ones?" Soren said. "Jatt and Jutt?"

"And Spoorn and Skench, and the wicked creatures of St. Aggie's. I dare not call them birds!"

"Was Zan the one who tried to rescue Hortense's egg?" Zan bobbed her head excitedly.

"Yes, indeed, and she did rescue it but it was on that mission that she lost her tongue," Streak explained.

Soren turned to Zan. "We saw you that terrible day. We saw what happened. You are both so brave to have helped Hortense."

"Hortense was the brave one. There was never an owl quite like Hortense. Do you know that in Ambala nearly every other newly hatched owl chick is being named Hortense, even if it's male?"

"Oh, my goodness!" Gylfie sighed. "And she hated the name so much. At least, that's what she told us."

"Well, a hero is known by one name now in the Kingdom of Ambala and that name is Hortense."

"What are you doing here in Kuneer?" Twilight asked.

"We fly patrol over Kuneer," Streak said, nodding at Digger. "We have a great liking for these desert creatures. While we were out hunting once, one of our little ones tried to fly before she was really ready. You know young ones. It's the one thing we always tell them not to do — don't try to fly too soon, never leave the nest when Da and Mum are away, and, bless my beak, don't a few always go and try it? She got a far piece but didn't know how to land and broke a small wing bone. One of these strange little owls, the ones that burrow in the sand, found our little Fiona and tucked her into their hole, fed her, coddled her, took the best care of her till her bone mended and she could fly. They found out where she came from and brought her back to us. Zan and I have always believed that there is more goodness than evil in the world. But you know, you still got to work at it. So that's what Zan and I do, now that all the little ones are gone. We work at it — doing good, that is."

Soren, Gylfie, Digger, and Twilight looked at the two large birds in wonder.

"I don't know how to thank you," Digger said.

Zan made a few nodding movements with her head that Streak observed carefully. "My dear mate says — you see, I can understand her even though she does not speak — Zan says that you must quit that foolish walking about in the desert all day and night. Too dangerous. What are you looking for so hard, my dear?"

"My family," Digger said. He then told Streak and Zan the story of what Jatt and Jutt had done to his brother Flick and how he had run off and was now lost.

Streak and Zan exchanged a long look. In that instant, Digger sensed that the two eagles knew his parents' fate. Zan stepped up to Digger and began preening his feathers with her beak in a soothing gesture. Streak took a deep breath. "Well, my son, I am afraid that we know what happened to your parents. You see, the feathers of the little brother you described were still there by the burrow and we saw your mum and da weeping mightily. So we asked what happened, and they told us how this had been their son Flick and they didn't know where in the world their two other young ones might be. Zan thought that this surely was the worst thing she'd ever heard. And though she can speak nary a sliver of a sound, she came back each day to preen your mother — to simply say in her own way 'I've been a mother, too, and though I have not lost a young one in this way I can feel how terrible it must be.'

"Then one day we got there a mite too late. The same two owls that nearly killed you just now came back for another run at the burrows and this time they came with reinforcements. There must have been fifty of them and they were wearing the most ferocious battle claws we'd ever seen. Well, we can take 'em on if there are only two or three in a war party, even with the claws, but fifty — no, no, that's no match."

"D-d-d-did . . ." Digger began to stutter. "Did they eat them?"

"No, just killed them. Said they were too tough and gristly."

There was a long silence now. No one knew what to say. Finally, Gylfie turned to Digger and spoke, "Come with us, Digger."

"But where is it you're going?" he asked.

"To the Great Ga'Hoole Tree."

"What?" said Digger, but before Twilight could answer, Streak broke in. "I've heard of that place, but isn't it just a story, a legend?"

"To some it might be," Twilight said, and blinked at the eagle.

But not to owls, thought Soren. *To owls,* he thought, *it is a real place.*

The dwenking moon had begun to slide down the bowl of the night. It hung like the curve of a talon low in the desert sky, spilling a river of silver across the land that seemed to flow directly to the four owls, lapping at the edges of their own talons. This light, flooding low and cool, seemed so different from the moon's scaldings and blinkings. It was a light that seemed to clear the mind and make bold the spirit. And something strange began to happen. Soren, with Mrs. P. on his shoulder, and Twilight and Gylfie stepped close to one another until their feathers were touching, and even Digger tucked in on the other side of Twilight. Where a short time before, Soren had wondered how he would explain his thoughts to the other owls, now he knew that no explanation was needed, that they had within the slivers of time and the silver of moonlight become a band. They were four owls who had lost their parents. But the time had come for them to become something else. They were not simply orphans. Together they were much more. Hadn't the Great Ga'Hoole Tree of the Ga'Hoollian Legends been the source of their greatest inspiration when they had been at St. Aggie's? Hadn't the Tales of Yore and the nobility of the knights of the Great Ga'Hoole Tree saved them from moon scalding? Could the legend become real? Could they, in fact, become part of the legend?

Soren's dream of Grimble was the worst sleeping dream he had ever had, but there was another dream, a waking dream that haunted the borders of Soren's mind and made his gizzard quiver. It was a dream that filled him with despair. In it, Soren was flying and spotted his parents perched in a tree. They had found a new hollow, and there was a brand-new nest lined with the fluffiest down. In the nest, there were new little owlets. Soren alighted on a limb. "Mum? Da? It's me, Soren." And his parents blinked, not in amazement but in true disbelief. "You're not our son," said his da. "Oh, no," said his mum. "Our son wouldn't look like you even grown up and fully fledged." "No," said his da, and both owls turned and ducked into the hollow. This, Soren realized in the deepest part of his gizzard, was why they had to go to the Great Ga'Hoole Tree. For when the world one knew began to crumble away bit by bit, when not only your memories but the memories that others might have of you grew dim with time and distance, when, indeed, you began to fade into a nothingness in the minds of the owls that you loved best, well, perhaps that was when legends could become real.

But at the heart of this nightmare was another deeper

truth. Soren had become something else. He turned slowly to look at the three other owls in the cool moonlight. Their eyes burned with a new intelligence, a new understanding. *Yes,* thought Soren, *and so had Gylfie and Twilight and Digger become something else.* No words were spoken. No words were needed. But a silent oath was sworn in that desert river of moonlight and the four owls all nodded. In that instant they knew that they were a band forevermore, bound by a loyalty stronger than blood. It was as a band they must go to Hoolemere and find its great tree that loomed now as the heart of wisdom and nobility in a world that was becoming insane and ignoble. They must warn of the evil that threatened. They must become part of this ancient kingdom of knights on silent wings who rose in the blackness to perform deeds of greatness.

And, indeed, Soren knew still another truth: Legends were not only for the desperate. Legends were for the brave.

"Let's go," said Soren.

"To Ga'Hoole!" cried Twilight.

"To Ga'Hoole!" echoed the others.

"All for owls and owls for all!" shouted Soren.

And in the still, deepest part of the night, four owls lifted into flight, their shadows printed on the hard desert sand below by the last spray of the moon's light. A Great

Gray flew in the lead, to windward a handsome Barn Owl, downwind flew a minute Elf Owl, in extremely quiet flight for such a talkative owl with no fringe on her feathers. Flying in the tail position, grappling with his talons across the windy wake of Twilight, flew Digger. All flew toward the River Hoole, which would empty into the great sea of Hoolemere, and an island where the Great Tree of Ga'Hoole grew and where, once upon a very long time ago, in the time of Glaux, there was an order of knightly owls who would rise each night into the blackness and perform noble deeds.

And Soren knew in his heart that now was the time for the legend to be true.

THE OWLS
and others
from

GUARDIANS of GA'HOOLE
The Capture

SOREN: Barn Owl, *Tyto alba*, from the kingdom of the Forest of Tyto; snatched when he was three weeks old by St. Aegolius patrols

> His family:
> KLUDD: Barn Owl, *Tyto alba*, older brother
> EGLANTINE: Barn Owl, *Tyto alba*, younger sister
> NOCTUS: Barn Owl, *Tyto alba*, father
> MARELLA: Barn Owl, *Tyto alba*, mother

> His family's nest-maid:
> MRS. PLITHIVER: blind snake

GYLFIE: Elf Owl, *Micrathene whitneyi*, from the desert kingdom of Kuneer; snatched when she was three weeks old by St. Aegolius patrols

TWILIGHT: Great Gray Owl, *Strix nebulosa*, free flyer, orphaned within hours of hatching

DIGGER: Burrowing Owl, *Speotyto cunicularius*, from the desert kingdom of Kuneer; lost in desert after attack in which his brother was killed by Jatt and Jutt

♭   ♭   ♭

SKENCH: Great Horned Owl, *Bubo virginianus*, the Ablah General of St. Aegolius Academy for Orphaned Owls

SPOORN: Western Screech Owl, *Otus kennicottii*, first lieutenant to Skench

JATT: Long-eared Owl, *Asio otus*, a St. Aegolius sublieutenant, warrior, and enforcer

JUTT: Long-eared Owl, *Asio otus*, a St. Aegolius sublieutenant, warrior, and enforcer; cousin of Jatt

AUNT FINNY: Snowy Owl, *Nyctea scandiaca*, pit guardian at St. Aegolius

UNK: Great Horned Owl, *Bubo virginianus*, pit guardian at St. Aegolius

GRIMBLE: Boreal Owl, *Aegolius funerus*, captured as an adult by St. Aegolius patrols and held as a hostage with the promise that his family would be spared

47-2: Western Screech Owl, *Otus kennicottii*, picker in the pelletorium of St. Aegolius

HORTENSE: Spotted Owl, *Strix occidentalis*, originally from the forest kingdom of Ambala, snatched at an indeterminate age by St. Aegolius patrols; trained as a broody owl in the eggorium of St. Aegolius

STREAK: Bald eagle, free flyer-

ZAN: Bald eagle, mate of Streak

A peek at
THE GUARDIANS *of* GA'HOOLE
Book Two: *The Journey*

They had left the hollow of the fir tree at First Black. The night was racing with ragged clouds. The tree covering was thick beneath them, so they flew low to keep in sight the river Hoole, which sometimes narrowed and only appeared as the smallest glimmer of a thread of water. The trees thinned and Twilight said that he thought the region below was known as The Beaks. And for a while they seemed to lose the strand of the river, and there appeared to be many other smaller threadlike creeks or tributaries. They were, of course, worried they might have lost the Hoole, but if they had their doubts they dared not even think upon them for a sliver of a second. For doubts, they all feared in the deepest parts of their quivering gizzards, might be like an owl sickness — like grayscale or beak rot — contagious and able to spread from owl to owl.

How many false creeks, streams, and even rivers had they followed so far, only to be disappointed? But now Digger called out, "I see something!" All of their gizzards quickened. "It's . . . it's . . . whitish . . . well, grayish."

"Ish? What in Glaux's name is ish?" Twilight hooted.

"It means," Gylfie said in her clear voice, "that it's not exactly white and it's not exactly gray."

"I'll have a look. Hold your flight pattern until I get back," said Twilight.

The huge Great Gray Owl began a power dive. He was not gone long before he returned. "And you know why it's not exactly gray and not exactly white?" Twilight did not wait for an answer. "Because it's smoke."

"Smoke?" The other three seemed dumbfounded.

"You know what smoke is?" Twilight asked. He tried to remember to be patient with these owls who had seen and experienced so much less than he had.

"Sort of," Soren replied. "You mean there's a forest fire down there? I've heard of those."

"Oh, no. Nothing that big. Maybe once it had been. But really, the forests of The Beaks are minor ones. Second-rate. Few and far between and not much to catch fire."

"Spontaneous combustion, no doubt," Gylfie said.

Twilight gave the little Elf Owl a withering look. Always trying to steal his show with the big words. He had no idea what spontaneous combustion was and he doubted if Glyfie did, either. But he let it go for the moment. "Come on, let's go explore," Twilight said.

They alighted on the forest floor at the edge of where the smoke was the thickest. It seemed to be coming out of a cave that was beneath a stone outcropping. There was a scattering of a few glowing coals on the ground and charred pieces of wood.

"Digger," Twilight said, "can you dig as well as you can walk with those naked legs of yours?"

"You bet. How do you think we fix up our burrows, make them bigger? We just don't settle for what we happen upon."

"Well, start digging and show the rest of us how. We've got to bury these coals before a wind comes up and carries them off and really gets a fire going."

It was hard work burying the coals, especially for Gylfie, who as the tiniest had the shortest legs of all. She and Mrs. Plithiver, who was not much more effective, worked as a team.

"I wonder what happened here," Gylfie said as she

paused to look around. Her eyes settled on what she thought was a charred piece of wood, but something glinted through the blackness of the moonless night. Gylfie blinked. The object glinted and curved into a familiar shape. Gylfie's gizzard gave a little twitch and, as if in a trance, she walked over toward it.

"Battle claws!" she gasped.

From inside the cave came a terrible moan. "Get out! Get out!"

But they couldn't get out! They couldn't move. Between them and the mouth of the cave, glowing eyes — redder than any of the live coals — glowered, and there was a horrible rank smell. Two curved white fangs sliced the darkness.

"Bobcat!" Twilight roared.

Out past the reach
of the Ga'Hoole Tree,
where survival is the
only law, live the
Wolves of the Beyond.

New from Kathryn Lasky

WOLVES OF THE BEYOND

In the harsh wilderness beyond
Ga'Hoole, a wolf mother hides in
fear. Her newborn pup has a twisted
paw. The mother knows the rigid
rules of her kind. The pack cannot
have weakness. Her pup must be
abandoned—condemned to die. But
the pup, Faolan, does the unthinkable.
He survives. This is his story—the story
of a wolf pup who rises up to change
forever the Wolves of the Beyond.

Kathryn Lasky has had a long fascination with owls. Several years ago, she began doing extensive research about these birds and their behaviors. She thought that she would someday write a nonfiction book about owls illustrated with photographs by her husband, Christopher Knight. She realized, though, that this would indeed be difficult since owls are shy, nocturnal creatures. So she decided to write a fantasy about a world of owls. Even though it is an imaginary world in which owls can speak, think, and dream, she wanted to include as much of their natural history as she could.

Kathryn Lasky has written many books, both fiction and nonfiction, including *Sugaring Time*, for which she won a Newbery Honor. Among her fiction books are *The Night Journey*, a winner of the National Jewish Book Award, and *Beyond the Burning Time*, an ALA Best Book for Young Adults, as well as the Daughters of the Sea and Wolves of the Beyond series. She has also received the Boston Globe-Horn Book Award and the Washington Post Children's Book Guild Award for her contribution to nonfiction.

Lasky and her husband live in Cambridge, Massachusetts.